Voyage
To
Mars

A Novel

by

Sir Patrick Moore,
CBE, FRS, DSc (Hon), FRAS

This novel is based upon a story I wrote over half a century ago, before even the first manned satellite, Sputnik I, was put in orbit by the Russians, and long before the idea of sending a manned mission to Mars was ever even contemplated.

Space travel developed, man went to the Moon, and voyaging to Mars is now a very real possibility.

So, fifty years on, as I enter my 80th year, I decided to re-write it and update it. I think it's a good story, and do you know - it could really happen.

Here is the result. I wonder how much updating it will need in, say, the year 2050?

Patrick Moore
Selsey, March 2003.

Front Cover illustration:
VOYAGE TO MARS
(Impression by Tony Wilmot.)

Published by **Belgrave Classics**
Windmill House, Windmill Road, St Leonards,
East Sussex, TN38 9BZ

1st Edition © Belgrave Classics 2003

Printed in Great Britain

Typeset by PROBOR
Printed in UK.

CHAPTER 1

THE TESTING GROUND

IT WAS almost three o'clock. The Sun blazed down from the blue Australian sky, shining upon the dead-white, ugly concrete roofs and the square brick buildings that made up the desert colony of Woomera. The heat was stifling, and to Maurice Gray, standing on the runway leading to one of the main rocket testing grounds, the air seemed as hot as a furnace.

Maurice was sixteen, fair-haired and slimly built. His grey eyes usually seemed to be laughing, but they were not laughing now. Seven months before, his parents had lost their lives in an air disaster, leaving him in the care of an old family friend who had also been their solicitor; only a few weeks later the solicitor too had died, and Maurice had been sent out to Australia to join his uncle, Leslie Yorke, who seemed to be his only surviving relation. All he knew about Yorke was that he was a well-known scientist working at Woomera Rocket Range, the great research station set up in the

Australian desert by the British and American Governments and now having a multi-national presence. Maurice had never met him, and nor did he do so when he arrived. Apart from an astronaut scientist named Bruce Talbot, who had gone out of his way to be friendly and whom Maurice liked at first sight, everyone seemed in fact to regard him as a nuisance. He had spent five days prowling round Woomera, or rather round as much of it as he was allowed to, and still Leslie Yorke had not appeared. It was not that the people of Woomera were exactly unfriendly; they were just indifferent, and already Maurice felt more lonely than he had ever done in his life.

He looked up, and saw Bruce Talbot coming along the concrete road towards him. Bruce was another puzzle. Only a few years older than Maurice, he seemed to hold a responsible position at Woomera, but he would never say just what it was, although Maurice knew he was a brilliant technician and of course an astronaut. He waved as he came up, but there was no smile upon his face, and his dark hair seemed even wilder and more untidy than usual.

'Haven't seen you for the last couple of days,' he said casually, taking off his sun-glasses and polishing them. 'How are you getting on? Still find us all a bit strange?'

Maurice shrugged. 'In a way. I wish I was a bit

older, that's all.'

Bruce looked at him keenly. 'What's up? Anything the matter?'

'Nothing in particular,' said Maurice wearily. 'It's... oh, I don't know. I guess I can't expect people here to take much notice of a school-kid from England, but I do wish I had someone to talk to every now and then.'

Bruce put a hand on his shoulder. 'I know. It's rough you're arriving just now. You couldn't have come at a worse time; if you'd been sent here six months ago, it'd have been very different. We're going through a tricky time at the moment, and you mustn't take any notice if we all seem a bit off-hand. It'll pass.'

Maurice looked round at the concrete buildings. In the distance he could hear a familiar sound - the roar of a rocket motor under test; otherwise all was silent, and he shook himself angrily.

'Look, have you got a few minutes to spare? If I don't chat to someone, I feel as though I'll burst!'

Bruce looked at his watch. 'I'm due down at the testing buildings in an hour, but you can take a stroll down with me if you like. You're not really allowed beyond the main gate, but it'll be all right if you come in with me, and it'll probably amuse you to see a rocket close at hand.'

Maurice nodded. 'Suits me,' he said, and fell into step as Bruce led the way in the direction of the main testing area. 'Can I ask you some questions?'

Bruce grinned. 'If you like. I can't guarantee to answer them, because a lot of what we do here is classified, but I'll tell you as much as I can. What do you want to know?'

'One thing in particular,' said Maurice bluntly. 'As you know, I was sent over here to be with my uncle, Dr. Yorke. I didn't expect him to come and meet me at the airport, or even when I first got to Woomera, but well, for Heaven's sake! I did think he'd see me pretty soon after I settled in. I've asked everyone I can find, and nobody will tell me a thing. All they'll say is that he's made arrangements for me to stay in the local school as soon as it opens for next term, and for the moment he's asked one of the engineers to put me up. Where is he? Is he in Woomera, or not? And why won't he come and see me?'

Bruce paused, and looked quickly at Maurice' s set face.

'It's... well, it's all rather odd,' he said slowly. 'He's not here at the moment, but as soon as he gets back I promise you he'll be only too glad to have you with him. He's a decent guy, in spite of his funny ways, and I know he was looking forward to your coming.'

'Where is he, then?' persisted Maurice. 'I know you're keeping something back. I'm sixteen, you know; I'm not a kid, and I don't want to make a nuisance of myself, but I do hate being kept in the dark.'

'I know,' said Bruce soberly. 'Trouble is, we've had to be so very careful here. There are a whole lot of people who would give a great deal to know just what we're up to, and we can't afford to run any risks.'

'In other words,' said Maurice bitterly, 'you don't trust me. All right, let it go. I won't pester you any more.'

'If you'll let me finish without jumping down my throat, I'll give you some of the answers, provided you give me your word that you won't talk about them once you're outside Woomera.' Bruce grinned. 'It's not a question of breaking any regulations, because I'm authorised to use my discretion; it's merely up to your common sense. Promise?'

'Need you ask?' said Maurice, drily.

'All right, then. Slow down a bit, or we'll reach the testing buildings before I've time to say all I've got to tell you.' Bruce slackened his pace. 'To begin with, I'll have to say something about Woomera itself - and it's a rather odd story. You know about the rockets used in the last war, of course?' Maurice nodded. 'Well, as soon as the war was over, the Americans began using rockets for scientific research, and so did the Russians. The main American base was at Cape Canaveral, in Florida, and of course it still is. That's the place they use for all their launches - and that goes for the shuttles to and from the International Space Station. The Russians had their rocket ground at Baikonur, which, believe me, is cold! I know, I've been there. Ever heard of it?'

'Yes, of course I have. What about this place then - Woomera?'

'Woomera was the British testing ground. We sent all our own experts out here, simply because we couldn't do much in a crowded country like England. That would also wake up the environmentalists, and they'd be down on us like a ton of bricks, so we chose a desert in the least populated part of Australia. At first, we all thought that Woomera would be as big as Canaveral. But it didn't work out that way.'

'Why not?'

'Two reasons: First, the Americans had all the money, and we hadn't. Then the British Government decided to go along with Canaveral instead of developing things here, and for a long time there was almost no activity in Woomera at all. It only started up again less than five years ago - when what's called nuclear-ion propulsion rockets started to come along. No way of testing those in Florida, so we got together with the Americans and others and decided on Woomera. It's working all right now, and of course your uncle is one of the leading lights.'

Maurice looked up sharply. 'I begin to see. If he's working on a space-ship of some sort, I don't wonder that he's been too busy to worry about me. Still, he might have left a message.'

'He did,' said Bruce shortly. 'He left it with me, which is why I'm able to tell you all this. He told me that I was to have a few talks with you and find out what sort of a guy you were, after which I could use my own judgement as to whether to tell you the whole story or not.'

There was a pause. 'Well?' said Maurice, at last. 'Do I pass?'

'I reckon so. Better get ready for a shock,' said Bruce, and hesitated. 'Well, you know that we're getting ready to set up proper bases on the Moon - that's been in the papers for some time - but there's more to it than that. So far most of the work has been done with the old-fashioned rockets - you know, step vehicles and boosters, much the same as the Apollo crews used long ago and with the Space Shuttle. But nuclear-ion propulsion rockets are much, much more powerful and take us further, and they'll soon take over. The snag is that we don't want part of a nuclear-ion engine to get into the wrong hands, like crazy terrorists, and we've got to be extremely careful.'

'I see,' said Maurice, thoughtfully. 'So Uncle Leslie's a nuclear-ion rocket man. Look, Bruce, what's all this leading to? You're keeping something back; I can see that. Where's my uncle now? You're not going to tell me he's on the Moon?'

'Not the Moon,' said Bruce calmly. 'Dr. Yorke's not a man to do things by halves. Several months ago, just about the time we first heard you were coming, he and his crew took off in the first nuclear-ion powered space-ship - bound for Mars.'

CHAPTER 2
THE *ARES*

FOR A few seconds Maurice's brain refused to take in what Bruce had said, and then the full realization of it came home to him almost like a blow. He blinked stupidly. This was the answer, then; his uncle had not met him because he was away not only from Woomera, but from the Earth itself. At this very moment, Leslie Yorke might be standing upon the dusty deserts of an alien planet, millions of miles away in space.

'I told you it would be a bit of a shock,' said Bruce quietly. 'Feel all right, kid?'

'Phew!' Maurice gave a breathless grin. 'I... I just can't believe it. Do you seriously mean that my uncle's up... up there?' He jerked his head towards the sky. 'How do you know he's still alive? I mean, anything may have happened to him. And how come it wasn't in the papers or media?'

'He was alive all right two days ago,' said Bruce drily. 'You seem to forget that there's such a thing as radio. Communication isn't particularly easy in outer space at great distances, because of solar and cosmic noise, but for a long time we had pretty regular messages, all scrambled on secret frequencies and utterly unintelligible to anyone outside Woomera. Your uncle's not alone, of course. There are two other astronauts with him - Professor Whitton, the naturalist, and a young American named Norman Knight, who's one of our leading experts in radar and navigation. As I told you, the last message came two days ago, when they were just about getting ready for the landing. And the Governments involved kept everything from the media because of the continuous and - it seems - ever growing threat of terrorism. Remember September 11th a while back in New York? Nuclear power is terrifying enough, especially if it were to be in the wrong hands, but nuclear-ion propulsion makes the power of a hydrogen bomb look like a firework cracker in comparison.'

Maurice drew a deep breath. 'But... but if they left six or seven months ago, surely they must have got to Mars by now?'

'Not a bit of it. Don't forget that even when it's at its very closest, Mars is still nearly forty million miles away. Moreover, you can't use the shortest path when you're travelling in a space-ship, so that it's a question of being out in space for months on end. If our calculations were correct, Yorke must have landed about nine days ago. There's a constant radio watch being kept, of course, and we'll be told as soon as anything comes through. As a back-up to voice radio, we've even gone back to using Morse code transmissions as an alternative method for communications to traverse the distances and interference.'

Maurice rubbed his eyes, still half-believing that he must be dreaming. 'So that's it,' he said, softly. 'Gosh - I wish I'd got here a few months ago, if I had to come at all. Why didn't you go with my uncle, Bruce? Weren't you keen?'

'I was extremely keen,' said Bruce, drily. 'There's nothing I would have liked better. As a matter of fact, the choice was narrowed down to about half a dozen astronauts. Radar and navigation are my strong points, and Norman Knight knows more than I do, so he got the job. I'll go next time, I hope.'

'There will be a next time, then?'

Bruce laughed. 'Sure. This is only the beginning. We've started setting up equipment on the moon, and before too long we'll have people there permanently, but you can't set up a really big colony. Mars may be a lot better, and if all goes well we may be able to turn it into a sort of second Earth. Remember, it's the first voyage that is the riskiest one. If your uncle comes back safely, more than half the problems will have been solved. Then, hopefully, the project can eventually all go public.'

Maurice's eyes wandered back to the gates of the testing area. 'I've so many questions to ask that I don't know where to begin. I thought that if you wanted to go to Mars, you'd start off from the Moon or a space-station.'

'Yes, if we had to use chemical rockets, but nuclear-ion power altered all that. No reason why I shouldn't show you the space-ship that we'll use for the next Mars trip. It's been under construction for the past year, and it's just about ready. Come on, then.'

He led Maurice through the iron gates with their printed notice: 'Danger - Keep Out', past the security guards, and down the long tarmac road that seemed to stretch into the far distance. This was the testing or 'proving' ground itself; there were no buildings apart from the steel and concrete structures, a long way ahead, and the ground was strangely barren, almost as though it had been scorched by flames. Maurice was busy with his thoughts. He was still trying to get used to the idea that his uncle was millions of miles away on another planet, and his brain was in a whirl. Bruce whistled absently as he walked, and for perhaps ten minutes they strode on, until the buildings were in full view.

'What's that circular thing over there with the tall gantry in the middle?' asked Maurice, at last. 'It looks almost like a huge pit.'

'It is. It's the main take-off platform,' said Bruce.
'The sides are made of reinforced concrete. When a
rocket first starts to climb, there's always the risk of an
accident, and in any case the heat generated is so
colossal that nobody can possibly stay near it. On the
other hand, we do want to see just how it behaves. Each
time there's an important ascent, five or six volunteers
get inside those concrete bunkers on the side of the
bowl - see them? - and there they stay. It's a risky
business. I've done it myself several times, and I like it
less each time I try it.'

'I don't wonder,' muttered Maurice. 'Have there
ever been any really bad accidents?'

'Yes, but we've been lucky,' said Bruce. 'We had a
scare a few months back, when an experimental rocket
blew up, and we might have lost a whole lot of people.
I could have been there myself.'

Maurice shivered. Somehow the air felt suddenly
chilly, despite the sticky heat, and he realized that
cutting-edge space research was not all 'fun and
games', whatever the story-books said. For a few
minutes he said no more; gradually they came up to the
buildings, and now they could see the huge strange
concrete and steel structures that seemed to be arranged
in a rough semicircle. Presently Bruce stepped off the
main path, and led the way across the rough ground in
the direction of the tallest of the buildings.

'You'll have to wait outside the fence,' he said,

pausing. 'David Mellor is the senior astronaut and the man in charge, and I'll have to get his permission before you can come inside the wired-in area. That's part of our routine, not because we want to keep to ourselves but because there are some compartments that are dangerously ionized or contain radioactive elements. I shan't be more than a few minutes.'

Maurice obediently halted by the side of the gates, by yet more security guards, and Bruce disappeared into the tall building, closing the entrance door after him. As a matter of fact, 'building' was a very inadequate word to describe the great structure, even though it did seem to be made mainly of steel rather than the usual steel and concrete. It was a full four hundred feet high, and cast a long shadow across the barren ground; it was windowless, and to one side of it bulged what looked almost like an aircraft hanger, with a curved roof.

The minutes passed slowly. Suddenly, the silence was broken by a shrill, harsh whine from the direction of the testing bowl gantry, and Maurice jumped. He had heard the same thing before, and knew it to be a rocket engine, but at comparatively close range it was loud enough to make him gasp and thrust his fingers into his ears. Gradually it faded away, and as it died into nothingness the silence that followed seemed almost terrifying. Maurice shook himself. 'Creepy sort of place,' he muttered, and wished that Bruce would return.

As a matter of fact, Bruce was rather longer than he had expected; a full half an hour passed before he reappeared, accompanied by a tall, lean man of perhaps thirty-five, wearing a white overall-coat and a pair of very ancient flannel trousers that were in urgent need of repair. This, evidently, was Dr. Mellor. Maurice rather liked the look of him. His bony face, with its pointed features and deep lines, seemed to show that at least he had a sense of humour.

'This is Gray,' said Bruce abruptly, as the two came up. 'Maurice, here's Dr. Mellor, my boss. He's given permission for you to have a look round, provided you do as you're told and don't poke your nose where you aren't allowed.'

'That's mainly for your own good,' said Mellor meaningly, crushing Maurice's hand in a vice-like grip that made him wince. 'One or two of our bits and pieces are dangerous, to say the least of it, and unless you want a dose of ion radiation poisoning you'd better be careful where you go. We've had several nasty accidents that way already, and we don't want any more, particularly at the present moment. I take it that what you really want to see is the *Ares*?'

'Is that the new space-ship, sir?'

'That's what I call her, anyhow,' said Mellor. 'I expect INASA - which you probably don't know is the InterNational Aeronautics and Space Administration -

the international branch of NASA - will christen her XYZ 1234, or something equally idiotic, but as I've been mainly responsible for her design I think I'm entitled to name her what I like. This way - and remember, don't go wandering off on your own.'

Maurice's first view of the *Ares* came as a distinct surprise. He had seen many of the American and European Space Agency launches on television, but Mellor's craft was quite different, and seemed to be made up of three parts joined loosely by inner sections, like gigantic flattened pears held together by a thick knitting-needle. Bruce chuckled.

'Not what you expected, eh?'

'Not a bit,' said Maurice, slowly. 'I... I didn't think a space-ship would be like that. It doesn't even have any wings, like the Shuttle.'

'Wings are pretty useless in space,' said Mellor. 'They're a great help when you're flying back into the Earth's atmosphere, and as a matter of fact the upper section of the *Ares* does have a pair rolled back into the main hull; but there's no air worth mentioning at above a height of a hundred and twenty miles, and it's well over forty million miles to Mars. See the bottom section?' Maurice nodded. 'Well, that holds the 'booster' motor. It's not atomic, and once it's lifted us up to a height of sixty miles or so it'll have done its job; it'll break free from the main body, and fall back to the ground by parachute. Then the main nuclear-ion motors in the second pear will take over.'

Maurice paused. 'Why, sir? I mean, why not use the main motors straight away?'

'For several reasons. First, the great thing about nuclear-ion power is that the combination removes any nasty nuclear radiation emissions from their use - that was the great breakthrough - otherwise a nuclear rocket would give off so much dangerous radiation that they would make all Woomera uninhabitable for a period of several months, and we certainly couldn't clear everybody out just because we wanted to make a test. But also they are so powerful and different it would attract all that attention we are trying to avoid. So, we use traditional Space Shuttle chemical rockets as a first stage. Their other strong point is that they can keep on providing power almost indefinitely, and once we're well away from the Earth it's persistence that counts rather than sheer brute force. When we take off from Mars, things will be much easier. Mars is much smaller than the Earth, so that it doesn't pull nearly so strongly, and I doubt whether anybody will mind if we scorch up a few square miles of Martian dust-desert, and of course there will be no-one around to see us.'

Maurice grinned. 'Nobody's waiting for us, then?'

'No little green men,' said Mellor. 'The atmosphere is much too thin for us to breathe, and it doesn't contain much oxygen, so we'll have to wear space-suits when we're in the open. There may have been fairly advanced life on Mars millions of years ago, but not now. If there's any life at all, it can't be as complicated as a blade of grass. The very most we can hope for is a few strips of mossy stuff although all the probes sent there over the years have never reported any life of any kind. It's a pity, but there it is.'

'Anyhow,' said Bruce seriously, 'we ought to know for certain within the next day or two. Unless anything's gone badly wrong, Dr. Yorke and his crew should be calling up any hour now.'

Mellor looked grave. 'To be candid, I'm starting to feel rather worried. When he last signalled, Leslie told us that he was preparing to land, and added that he'd call up again as soon as he was safely down. I wish he'd do it, that's all.'

'You don't think he's crashed?' muttered Maurice

'Not really. Radio and space-ship telemetry communication is bound to be difficult, and in any case we haven't the slightest idea whether it will be possible for him to get in touch with us when he's actually on Mars. The air there is queer stuff - the last probe that landed there discovered that there was some kind of moving 'layer', which we call the 'Violet Layer', about which we know practically nothing at all - and it may block out radio signals entirely. All I'm saying is that I shall feel a good deal happier in my mind when we've had some definite news.' Mellor turned to Maurice. 'I don't want to seem unfriendly, Gray, but I've a great

deal of work to do, and I shall want Bruce's help. Once
we've reached the stage when we could take off at a
moment's notice if necessary, things will be much
easier.'

Bruce looked at Maurice. 'Satisfied for the moment,
kid?'

'I don't want to get in the way,' said Maurice, and
stepped towards the door. 'Thanks for showing me the
Ares, sir. I only wish I was a bit older, so that I could
come with you.' Mellor chuckled inside - it takes many
years to train up astronauts like himself, a veteran of
several Shuttle missions... 'Shall I find my own way
out?'

'I'll come with you as far as the main gates - if
you're not wanting me for a few minutes, David?' said
Bruce, and Mellor nodded. 'There's one thing more I
can show you as we go, and that's the Communications
Centre. We've kept a twenty-four hour watch ever
since Dr. Yorke started out, and there are people on duty
there all the time.'

'No harm in that,' said Mellor. 'He can even listen
in for a few minutes, if he's interested. In any case, I
shall have to check over those computer units before we
can start signing them off, and that'll take me several
hours yet. Come back as soon as you're ready.' He
turned back on his way across to the great space-craft.
'Don't take too much notice of what I said just now,
young Gray. If any man can take care of himself, it's

Leslie Yorke; and if we don't have some sort of a message from him during the next couple of days, I for one will be very much surprised.'

CHAPTER 3

A MESSAGE FROM MARS

THE TALL masts and huge radio telescope dishes seemed to reach towards the sky, making a landmark that could be seen from any part of the Station. The Communications Centre at Woomera lay well away from the main proving ground, across a full half-mile of the rough, barren country; the buildings themselves were of steel and brick, and outside stood a number of large wire dish instruments that were utterly unlike anything Maurice had seen before. He blinked at them.

'What on earth are those?'

'Radio telescopes,' said Bruce briefly. 'You know that the stars send out radiations of all wavelengths, don't you? They give off radio waves as well as light, and those telescopes pick them up.'

Maurice rubbed his chin. 'You don't mean you can tune in to the Pole Star and listen to a rock band?'

'Not quite,' said Bruce, with a chuckle. 'All you'll get is a radio signal which is transferred to a computer screen. The radiations are called 'radio' signals, but you certainly can't hear them. See that building over there, below the aerials? That's where we've installed our most powerful receivers, and that's where Hayley Daniels and her assistants are keeping a watch on Dr. Yorke's communication and telemetry frequencies.'

Maurice said no more, but followed Bruce into the Communications Centre, looking curiously round him at the various instruments, computers and huge display screens. He had seen many shots of such a scene before, on television in connection with Space Shuttle missions. They passed through a room almost filled with a tremendous machine that seemed to be one mass of dials, switches and screens; along a corridor; through another room crowded with apparatus, and finally into a much larger hall, with complicated equipment in the middle and more computer screens all round. A soft hissing noise could be heard, and Maurice's eyes fell upon two men and one woman, two of them wearing headsets and the third checking the systems themselves.

'Any luck, Hayley?' asked Bruce, quietly.

The woman at the desk turned. 'Not a squeak,' she said, in what was unmistakably an American accent. 'Either that damned planet stops them getting through, or else Norman's made a hash of the radio. The messages are ninety hours overdue by now. Hi, who's the kid?'

'Yorke's nephew - Maurice Gray,' said Bruce, and

Maurice shook hands, with an inward feeling of resentment at the way that everyone called him a 'kid'. 'Look, Hayley, I've got to get back and help Mellor finish checking the radar equipment on the *Ares*. Do you mind if Maurice listens in for a bit?'

The American shrugged. 'All right by me, but we've about given up on the voice channels and are into Morse - so what's the use if he can't read Morse? Not that he's likely to hear much anyway, unless you count solar crackle,' she added. 'I don't reckon Yorke will call up again until he's well on his way home.'

'I can read Morse,' said Maurice. 'At least, I passed a test at twenty words a minute just before I left school in England. It was part of the fun of an engineering club at the school.'

Hayley raised her eyebrows. 'Good for you. That's about the most useful thing I've heard UK GCSE schools do for anyone. There you are, kid - all those headsets are connected up. If you want to make yourself useful, you can take your turn in listening out. We always have two CAPCOM operators on duty together for this mission, just in case one of them falls asleep!'

Bruce went out, and Maurice put on the headset and settled down. At first, all he could hear was a roar that sounded like distant water. He adjusted the volume control on the console, and presently he could make out sharp 'pinging' noises against the background, while now and then came a high-pitched whistle. This, evidently, was the 'solar noise', due to radiations sent out by the Sun itself. After a time he became more or less used to the din, but it struck him that it would be very difficult to pick up feeble Morse signals under such conditions. Ten minutes passed, and Hayley came over to him, grinning.

'Having fun, kid?'

Maurice unplugged his headset from his ear. 'I guess it'd make your head ache like crazy after an hour or two,' he said ruefully. 'Is it always as bad as this?'

Hayley shook her head. 'No. It's noisy when the Sun's above the horizon, because then you're getting the worst of the solar interference. We do keep a watch all the time, but I don't think we'd have a chance of picking up any signals except after dark. As a matter of fact, Mars is high in the sky now, so we can't afford to slack. Had enough?'

'Not me. I'd like to carry on, if that's all right with you,' said Maurice, and replaced his headset. 'It's a lot better than loafing around Woomera trying not to get in the way.'

There was a long pause. Maurice kept on the alert, and gradually, so it seemed, the solar crackling grew less insistent; the 'pinging' sounds faded, and so did the whistles, until the deafening noise had died away to little more than a loud hiss. He glanced at his watch, and saw to his surprise that over three hours had passed

since he had first come into the Communications
Centre. It must be getting near sunset. He strained his
ears, and listened intently for the slightest sound of
anything unusual. Again there was a long pause, and
then - suddenly, and much to his astonishment - he
heard something.

Maurice breathed hard, and turned up the volume
control. Was he imagining things? No - very faintly,
very uncertainly, he could hear the well-known dot-
dash signals that made up the Morse code, and he gave
a shout.

'Listen! They're... they're here!'

Hayley made a bound towards the radio, and thrust
on a headset; the second operator, too, was already on
the alert, leaning forward and concentrating grimly in
an attempt to understand the blurred, distorted signals.
As Hayley made the computers work to enhance the
sound the Morse grew stronger, until it could be read
without difficulty:

'Yorke calling Woomera. Yorke calling Woomera.
Reply. Over.'

Hayley breathed hard, switched the transmitter to
full power and sent a Morse message flashing back.
'Woomera calling Yorke. Woomera calling Yorke.
Receiving you. Over.'

There was a long silence, and Maurice's hands
gripped the table until his knuckles showed white.
Then Yorke's original message was repeated, but

Hayley made no move to reply. Maurice gave a hoarse whisper: 'Can't they hear us?' Hayley saw his lips move, and lifted her headset for a moment. 'Don't worry. Radio waves take time to travel, you know, and Mars is a long way off. We shan't get any reply for another four minutes yet, even if he's picked us up. Keep listening.'

Maurice strained. The minutes passed, and then he tensed as the Morse dot-dashes came through again:

'Yorke calling Woomera. The *Hermes* has landed in latitude 10° north, longitude 310° - repeat, latitude 10° north, longitude 310°. Our landing was faulty. Rocket is damaged beyond repair. Repeat, rocket is damaged beyond repair. Have managed to erect transmitter, but shall be unable to call again after next few hours. Can hold out for eight to nine months only. Repeat, can hold out for eight to nine months only. We are...'

Abruptly, the Morse stopped. Hayley pressed the transmitter key, and sent a reply flashing into space; then she turned to the second operator, and motioned him to take off his headset.

'Steve, you'd better rustle round and collect the gang. All of them - Mellor and Talbot from the *Ares*, Joan Lindsdell and Shelley Harrington from the gravity department, Schwarz, Haller and the rest - Sir Robert, too. They'll all want to be in on this one. I'll keep listening out, and see if I can get them again.

'Right,' rapped the CAPCOM, and was gone almost

before Hayley had finished speaking. Maurice strained his ears... Was that a signal? No; nothing but the ever-present hiss, and he looked inquiringly at Hayley.

'What's gone wrong?' he breathed.

'How do I know? They've messed up their landing, and I reckon they must have damaged their radio as well. Well, it's the finish for them,' said Hayley grimly. 'I hope to goodness they manage to get through just once more and tell us what happened, or else the next expedition may go the same way. Lord! To think of it! There they are on Mars, with a smashed space-ship, waiting for their air to run out... I may be yellow, but I'm sure glad I'm not with them.'

Maurice swallowed hard. The prospect of waiting for months, with the knowledge that only death lay in store, made him feel physically sick, and he shook himself angrily in an effort to keep a grip on himself. Again Hayley called, but no reply came from across the millions of miles of space, and he shrugged helplessly. At last Bruce came in, looking white and strained; Mellor followed, and then a number of others, most of whom Maurice had never seen before.

'Anything new?' said Mellor, quietly.

Hayley shook her head. 'Not a bite, sir. This is the lot.' She passed over a computer printout. 'They broke off in the middle of a sentence. It's my guess that we won't hear anything more from them - ever.'

Mellor read quickly through the message. 'Eight to

nine months,' he muttered. 'What the hell do they mean by a faulty landing? Leslie's not the man to make a miscalculation and the telemetry was fine until we lost contact; there must be some unknown factor... What do you make of it, Bruce?'

'The same as you,' said Bruce shortly. 'They've given us a position, at least, and we know that they've come down in the middle of the dust desert Aeria, but that's not much help. If only we had something more to go on! What are we going to do?'

'I know what I'd like to do,' said Mellor, without hesitation, 'and if I'm given half a chance I'm going to do it. Where the devil is Sir Robert?'

Maurice had never seen Sir Robert Lanner, Chief Controller of Woomera Research Station, but he had heard all about him. His strong, bearded face, with its bushy eyebrows and ice-cold eyes, was well known to everybody who read the newspapers or watched television. Sir Robert was reputed to be the most brilliant physicist of his day, and he was also said to be a man who never altered his mind once he had come to a decision. It was Sir Robert who had been responsible for the linking-up of Woomera with the American research department at Canaveral, and he too who had gathered together all the cleverest space scientists in the world, so that the knowledge gained from their work could be pooled without a scrap of it being wasted. When he came into the room a few seconds later, he seemed almost to fill it, though physically he was not a big man, and when he spoke it was in a deep voice that somehow made Maurice feel more confident.

'This is a bad business,' said Sir Robert, without preamble. 'I may tell you that I happened to be listening in on my personal squawk box, so you need waste no time in telling me just what Yorke said.' His gaze wandered round the room. 'I am glad to see that your team has been wise enough to continue recording and listening out, Miss Daniels, even though I doubt whether we shall hear any more. Dr. Mellor, have you any theories as to the cause of this disaster?'

Mellor ruffled his lank black hair. 'I wish I had. As I told Talbot just now, Yorke's much too clever and cool an astronaut to make any fool errors of judgement. There's some unknown factor connected with Mars itself; and unless we can find out what it is, the next expedition is likely to fall into the same trap. It may be that the surface is unsafe; it may be the roaming Violet Layer in the atmosphere; it may be that the gravitational field has something odd about it that we just didn't know - it's impossible to tell.'

'Quite so.' Sir Robert turned to Bruce. 'Have you anything to say from the point of view of radar and navigation astronautics, Mr. Talbot?'

Bruce shrugged helplessly. 'No, sir. I haven't a clue. We'll go on trying to pick them up again, of course.'

'That goes without saying,' said Sir Robert impatiently. 'Well, ladies and gentlemen, I imagine that none of us fails to see the full significance of this message from the *Hermes*. Yorke, Whitton and Knight are stranded fifty million miles away, with a space-craft that is clearly crippled and a radio that has ceased to function. We know where they are; if the position they gave us is correct, the *Hermes* is lying in the desert of Aeria, some way from the borders of the dark tracts of the Syrtis Major and the Deltaton Sinus. They say that they can keep alive for at least eight months, but unless we can help them within that time they will die from lack of air and water. Are there any comments? Professor Haller?'

The Danish engineer polished his gold-rimmed spectacles. 'It is difficult, Sir Robert - it is most difficult. Ach, we have the tied hands. One ship only we have, the *Ares*. Four men alone can it carry, and three are needed for the voyage. It will perhaps be possible to send Yorke the supplies...'

Mellor broke in. 'How, Axel? You're not suggesting that we should fire off some sort of probe, and trust that we can get it down in exactly the right spot? You know as well as I do that there's not one chance in ten million that we could land it on Mars with that degree of accuracy for the *Hermes*. Besides, it's not food they want - it's air. If their nuclear-ion internal environmental systems have been damaged, as seems entirely possible, their oxygen plant may not be working perfectly, and so their oxygen won't last them for more than nine months at the outside.'

Haller shrugged. 'I know, my friend. You misunderstand. We could perhaps put the *Ares* in a path round Mars, and from their make the operations? We would need to build the special equipment, but it might perhaps be attempted.'

'Let us be practical,' said Sir Robert quietly. 'There are only two possibilities open to us. Either a crew could man the *Ares* and make an effort to reach Yorke, or else we could try to send supplies on their own. To build a supply rocket would take months, even if we worked day and night and pooled all resources with NASA at Canaveral; it would be out of the question to get it ready in time to follow up Professor Haller's suggestion. On the other hand, it would take even longer to build another *Ares*, and in her present form the *Ares* herself cannot carry more than four men. Three are needed to handle the blast-off so that only one extra passenger could be brought back from Mars.'

There was a long silence.

'In other words,' said Mellor, 'we couldn't rescue more than one of them, even if we could use the *Ares* and get her there in time. That's what you mean, sir, isn't it?'

'Yes.' Sir Robert's voice was cold and unemotional. 'Remember, Dr. Yorke and his companions are astronauts. They knew the dangers they were running, and they would not expect others to throw their lives away on a useless mission. If a rescue party were to get to them in time, it would have to start within the next week or so, which would mean cancelling all the final tests - of which there are many - that should still be made. You know as well as I do that it is impossible for the *Ares* to blast off with a crew of less than three, and equally impossible for it to return with more than four. Are we justified in wrecking the work of many years merely to take a mad gamble upon rescuing one man? We may as well be frank with ourselves. There is nothing we can do.'

Mellor leaned forward. 'You don't mean that we've got to sit back here and do nothing? Damn it, sir, those men can manage on their own for months yet. There must be something!'

Sir Robert shrugged. 'What, Dr. Mellor?'

'Let me think,' said Mellor savagely. 'Thank Heaven, I spent most of last week making some new calculations with regard to mass ratios and the weight that could be carried, and I'm not sure that we couldn't take a crew of five provided that we stripped the *Ares* of everything except the bare essentials. We couldn't even think of it on the outward trip, but it's possible that we might manage it on the return - we'd only have to work up to three miles a second instead of seven. Every ounce would matter.'

'Even so,' said Sir Robert, 'one of Yorke's crew would still have to be left behind. Be reasonable, Mellor. I am responsible to Governments for this whole programme of research, and without a good chance of rescuing all of Yorke's crew - not merely one or two of them - I wouldn't feel justified in throwing away our one remaining space-craft and three more of our best men and women. We haven't only ourselves to consider; the whole development programme at Woomera would be thrown into question.'

Mellor leaned forward. 'Aren't you forgetting something, Sir Robert? We know that unless Yorke made a mistake, which isn't likely, there is some danger waiting for us on Mars. If we can get to him before he dies, we can find out what it is. If not, the next expedition will go the same way.'

Sir Robert paused. 'I admire your attitude, Mellor. And what you have just said is a most valid point. Believe me, I don't like the idea of doing nothing, and waiting for them to suffocate, any more than you do - probably less, because in the final reckoning I'm ultimately responsible for the mission. Well, what do you want to do?'

'If you'll ask me that again in twenty-four hours,' said Mellor, 'I'll tell you. With your permission, I'm going back to the *Ares*. My team will check every possible thing we can, strip her down to the bare bones, and re-calculate. If I reckon I can bring all three of them back, will you give me leave to try it?'

There was a long silence.

'As you said just now,' said Sir Robert, 'every ounce will count. That would mean the *Ares* being manned by the three lightest people available. I'll go this far, Mellor; I'll postpone my decision until you've had time to do all the checking you want. Will that satisfy you?'

Mellor nodded. 'Thank you, sir. Will you come down to the take-off platform at - let me see - at six o'clock tomorrow? Bruce, I shall want you to help me; Haller, too. There's not a moment to lose.'

The next twenty-four hours seemed to whirl by. Nobody took any notice of Maurice, and he followed Mellor and Bruce back to the proving ground, waiting near the entrance to the great building and listening to the sounds of feverish activity going on inside. The sun had set by now; the stars glowed down from the velvety black sky, and Maurice stared upwards, his thoughts millions of miles away. There was the Southern Cross, shining brilliantly from the midst of the Milky Way; there was the glorious star Canopus; and there, too, was a bright reddish light that seemed almost to show a tiny disk. Maurice fixed his eyes upon it. Mars - the Red Planet! At this moment, three Earthmen waited helplessly upon its surface, wondering what their friends could do to come to their aid, powerless to save themselves and utterly dependent upon the calculations that Mellor and his team were making in a building fifty million miles distant.

At exactly 6pm the following evening, Maurice stood again at the same spot. He realized that Sir Robert had passed through the main door, and his heart beat furiously. Any moment now, they would know whether it was possible to take a desperate gamble, or whether Yorke and his friends would have to be left to a lingering death... And then, suddenly, he heard his name being called. It was Mellor's voice, and without pausing to think Maurice ran towards the open door.

'I'm here, sir.' He pulled up, and blinked in the brilliant glare of the electric lights. 'What... what's happened?'

'So far,' said Mellor, 'nothing.' He paused, and Maurice became aware that he was being watched closely not only by Bruce, but also by Sir Robert and the many other scientists and technicians in the room. 'Listen carefully, boy. How much do you weigh?'

Maurice stammered, very conscious of his slight, spare body. About, about a little under seven and a half stone, sir. Why?'

'Seven and a half stone - 105 pounds,' breathed Mellor, and turned to Sir Robert. 'You hear that, sir? That's less than any of the female astronauts here or at Canaveral. We can do it - by the skin of our teeth!'

'Not so fast,' said the Chief Controller, curtly. 'You're too ready to rush into things, Mellor. I'm not at all sure that I've any right to let you carry out this mad scheme of yours...'

Mellor broke in unceremoniously, and gripped Maurice by the shoulder. 'I don't suppose you've any idea what I'm driving at, but I'm not going to beat about the bush. What we have to do is to take off with three aboard, and come back with six. Because of the uniqueness of the *Ares* and its systems, Bruce and I have to go. It'll be a risky business, to put it mildly, and unless our original crew weigh less than thirty stone between them we've no chance of success. I weigh eleven stone, Bruce nine, and you seven and a half. That's twenty-seven and a half stone altogether - 385 pounds. You know something about radio, and if you sweat night and day until we launch off you can be taught all that's required of you. It's worth the gamble, Gray - if you've courage enough to come with us!'

Maurice gave a gasp. For a moment his brain would not work. Mellor's words seemed too incredible and then he realized that he was answering, his voice harsh and strained.

'I'm with you, sir. I... I'll do my best not to let you down.'

Mellor swung round on Sir Robert. 'Well, sir? If a kid of sixteen is willing to take the chance, you can't refuse to let us try it.'

'I know,' said Sir Robert curtly. 'All my scientific training is dead against it, but you've forced my hand. You realize what you're up against, and the chances of your coming back safely, with or without Yorke, are pretty small, but I've no choice. Very well, Mellor. Officially, I think the three of you are crazy fools, but I'll recommend it up above and get the Governments to run with it; unofficially - good luck, and Heaven be with you!'

CHAPTER 4
LIFT-OFF

MAURICE FELT deathly tired, and rubbed his eyes wearily. He stared up at the towering body of the *Ares*, transferred now from the building in which it had been created into the main take-off bowl of the base and attached by various cables and locking arms to the steel gantry. For a few minutes, at least, there was nothing that he need do, and he was in real need of a rest.

Five days had passed since Sir Robert and the Heads of Government, pushed by Sir Robert to agree the very same day he consulted them, had come to the 'GO' decision - five days of feverish activity throughout Woomera. In the buildings, Mellor had worked twenty-four hours at a stretch, checking, assembling and calculating, with Bruce and Axel Haller and a gang of engineers and research scientists and technicians. The communications department had been unwearying in its efforts to re-establish contact with the stranded astronauts, but so far without success, and with every hour the chances grew slimmer. 'I guess their radio has packed in altogether,' Hayley had said on one of the many occasions when Maurice was learning radio and communications with her. Maurice had proved to be a fast and intelligent student; his knowledge had increased considerably and his Morse speed grown to an excellent professional standard. 'They could also run off the main storage batteries, remember, and if those were damaged too during the landing it'd cut down their power so much they wouldn't have a hope of calling us again.' Nor had Sir Robert himself been idle. Few people appreciated the full extent of his knowledge, but now and then Mellor or Haller would call for his help, and they never called in vain. Maurice had also been handed over to Professor Joan Lindsdell, the head of the Physics Department, for a course in what Mellor called 'astronautics and instrument control'. Lindsdell was a good tutor, and before long Maurice had achieved a wide understanding of the mission and deft skill at handling his assigned duties. He also knew much more generally of what lay in store for him. One thing that Lindsdell told him always stuck in his memory.

'You know,' she had said, leaning back in her chair and looking quizzically at Maurice from behind her thick-lensed spectacles, 'some people are stupid enough to believe that we've learned so many of the secrets of nature that we're almost ready to unlock the key to the door of universal knowledge. That is pure idiocy. We know less about the universe than an Australian aborigine knows about the London docks. We don't know exactly what you're going to find on Mars, assuming you do get there safely; I don't personally think you'll find life of any kind whatsoever, but one never knows. In other words, you've got to be ready for anything. How do you feel about that - are you scared?'

At the time Maurice had protested that he did not feel in the least frightened, but now that the great adventure was so nearly beginning he had to admit to himself that he felt apprehensive inside. For one thing, he hated the idea of 'zero gravity'. Out in space, once the rocket had worked up to a speed sufficient to break free from the powerful pull of the Earth, he would weigh nothing at all, simply because he would be travelling at the same speed and in the same direction as the *Ares* itself; and his experiences in the experimental gravity chamber installed in the main physics laboratory had been far from reassuring. The first few times, he had been horribly sick, and had emerged feeling more ill than he had ever done in his life. Later on, things had improved somewhat, but he knew that six months in a space-ship would be a very different matter from a few hours spent intermittently in a gravity chamber.

'Well?' said a familiar voice, and Maurice turned to find Bruce by his side. 'We've not long to go now, thank goodness. Lift-off's timed for 7.30, which is less than ten hours. Feel nervy?'

Maurice forced a grin. 'In a way, but I'm not thinking of backing out, if that's what you're getting at! I only wish I'd had a bit longer to get the hang of all the instruments and computer systems.'

'I know,' said Bruce soberly. 'It's asking a hell of a lot to expect you to learn the whole set-up in less than a week. If it's any comfort to you, though, I've been talking to Lindsdell and Daniels, and they say you've done wonders. Frankly, you're the least of our worries.'

Maurice shrugged. 'I'm glad you think so. I feel completely washed out. Wonder where we'll be this time to-morrow?'

'A good many thousands of miles out in space, I hope,' said Bruce. 'Well, there isn't much more we can do for the moment. If there are any faults left in the *Ares* now, we can't find them. What you'd better do is to go back and have something to eat - I'd like to come with you, but I haven't time - and then make your way back here. Incidentally, I believe Sir Robert wants a word with you.'

Maurice looked up quickly. 'He hasn't found someone to take my place?'

Bruce chuckled. 'Don't worry, there's still no other astronaut, male or female, who weighs as little as you; it's nothing like that. Off you go. Don't eat too much, or you'll put on a stone too many!'

As a matter of fact, Maurice felt far too strung-up to eat much. If the previous five days had flown by, these last hours seemed to drag. All Woomera was very quiet, and an old catch-phrase flitted through his mind: 'the calm before the storm'. He wondered just what form the storm would take.

Over the past few days he had also come to realize just how astonishingly advanced the technology of the *Ares* really was. With the chemical and liquid-fuel rockets used at Canaveral, especially the Space Shuttle, everything was automatic; the idea that a space-craft could take off 'on its own' - independent of the mass of ground computers and personnel - was new, but essential of course for a space-ship which had to travel fifty million miles, land on an alien planet and take off again. It also meant that everything had to be continuously monitored by those on board, and Maurice knew that he would be tested to the utmost during the lift-off. The *Ares* was as different from a shuttle vehicle as the shuttle had been from the crazy contraptions first flown well over a hundred years earlier.

It was 5pm when he arrived back at the launch site, and by that time Mars was shining brightly down from the darkening sky almost as though it were mocking him. As he came up to the take-off bowl, feeling very small and decidedly nervous, he saw the bearded figure of Sir Robert Lanner, and he paused.

'Did you want to see me, sir?'

Sir Robert turned. 'Yes, Gray. I want to make quite sure that you understand not only the details of this mission but also - and more importantly - the risks you're running. The bottom line is: this mission might fail and you might die. You have to face that, and I feel very concerned that, as you are only sixteen, it's a fact that should be made very clear to you. Have you any last-minute hesitations, and do you want to pull out? If so, frankly, everyone would understand completely.'

Maurice listened quietly as Sir Robert continued.

'I must tell you, I think you've less than one chance in ten of coming back. The very fact that Yorke has come to grief shows that there are some things which we have failed to take into account. I've just been talking to Mellor and Talbot, and they seem perfectly ready to put their trust in you, but if you've any doubts in your mind about them or the mission itself, it's only fair to you to be given the opportunity to draw back now before it's too late.'

'I haven't any doubts, sir,' said Maurice steadily. 'I know this is the right thing to be doing, and I believe we have a chance of pulling it off - and if we don't, well, it won't be for want of trying.'

Sir Robert looked at him sharply, and then gave a surprisingly human smile. 'All right, boy. That's what I hoped you'd say. If you do 'pull it off', as you put it, I imagine your uncle will have every reason to be proud of you. Well, all I can say is 'good luck'. Mellor and

Talbot are inside the *Ares* now, and you'd better join them.'

He crushed Maurice's hand, and moved away without waiting for a reply. Haller came up and said something; Lindsdell was there too, and Hayley Daniels, and Maurice felt that all eyes were upon him as he walked firmly up to the waiting space-ship.

Now that she was in the open, unprotected by the steel housing building, the *Ares* looked even more grotesque than before. The three flattened pears that made her up were unequal in size, the bottom one being the largest, the second or nuclear-ion pear rather smaller, and the top one - the crew cabin - the smallest of all. Maurice entered the gantry lift with three technicians and, as the lift rose quickly, tried not to look down in case he should feel giddy. 'I'd look an idiot if I was sick now, and no mistake,' he muttered to himself, and hung on doggedly. At last he had reached the top, and walked along the walkway to the entrance to the cabin, and a moment later he was safely inside the main air-lock.

During the past five days, in addition to his experiences in the flight simulator, he had paid several visits to the craft that was to be his home for the next few months, and he knew what to expect. The outer door did not open straight into the cabin; it led into a small room, hardly large enough to hold more than one person, which itself led into another room of equal size.

Each air-lock had tightly-fitting doors, and it was possible to exhaust the air by drawing it back into the main body of the *Ares* by a system of pumps, thus avoiding the loss of precious oxygen each time one of the crew went in or out. Oxygen, Maurice had learned, was the all-important thing. There was no difficulty in carrying food supplies sufficient to last for years, if necessary, but the life-giving gas had to be strictly controlled, even though the nuclear-ion systems could re-generate oxygen from the carbon dioxide gas exhaled by each astronaut.

The main cabin itself was circular, and far from roomy. In the centre was a massive pillar, set in which were the main computers and instrument panels, and radiating outwards from it, like the legs of a starfish, were four comfortable-looking, heavily sprung couches. The communications console occupied almost a quarter of the remaining space, and there was also a chart table, though Maurice knew by now that navigating a space-ship was very different from steering an aircraft; almost everything was done by computer and radar, and made as nearly automatic as possible. Both Bruce and Mellor were waiting, making last-minute checks of the various pieces of equipment, and Bruce looked up as Maurice stumbled in.

'We were wondering if you'd got cold feet at the last moment,' he said; and laughed at Maurice's expression. 'All right, pal - I didn't mean it! Are you ok?'

'So far,' said Maurice, and went over to the radio. 'Any last-minute orders, sir?'

'Not from me,' said Mellor, 'except that I forbid you to call me 'sir' any more!' Maurice grinned.

'You know what to do,' continued Mellor. 'Your job is to give me the instrument readings whenever I want them, which will probably be every ten seconds or so while we're accelerating, and also to take over the radio as soon as we've jettisoned the first stage and cut our motors. You'd better get started and run your pre-launch checks.'

Maurice obeyed. The radio itself was perfectly easy to handle, but he now knew only too well that nothing must be left to chance, and the entire complex communications systems had to be monitored and checked frequently. He accessed the main control, and satisfied himself that communications - voice and Morse - were in perfect order, after which he studied the mass of dials, switches, screens and indicators, running his pre-flight checks as he had been trained. Now that the moment of lift-off was so near, he was no longer nervous, even though he could not help wondering whether this was all some strange dream.

'Right,' said Mellor at last, stepping back and running his hands through his untidy hair. 'Sixty minutes to go. We'd better strap down.'

Bruce and Maurice nodded, and fastened themselves securely into the sprung couches, shifting about until they had found the most comfortable positions, and swinging their hinged instrument panels within easy reach. Mellor followed suit. They spent the next while carrying out their last routine checks; finally, Mellor turned to Maurice.

'Call up again. Tell them we're all set.'

Maurice flicked on the transmitter, and fixed his headset. 'Hello, Control. *Ares* calling Woomera Control. We are all positioned, final checks are complete and we are preparing for lift-off. T minus six minutes and counting.' The familiar 'bleep' sound followed Maurice's transmission.

'Control calling *Ares*. T minus six minutes confirmed. Stand by for a message.' There was a pause, and Maurice switched over to open speakers; then Sir Robert's voice came to them: 'Lanner here. I want to say: we all know that this is not the easiest of missions, but I do believe that there have never been three astronauts with more courage and determination than you have all shown over the last week. Good luck to you. God speed - we wish you well.'

'Thank you, sir,' said Mellor, crisply. 'We'll give it the best shot we can.'

Five minutes... four... three... Maurice felt his skin prickling; Bruce and Mellor lay still, apparently quite unmoved by the thought that they were about to be hurled into space at the terrifying speed of seven miles a second. Two minutes... one...

'Stand by,' said Mellor. 'T minus thirty seconds.'

Maurice heard himself counting out loud. He could see Mellor's hand hovering over the Master Launch control switch, and braced himself, the sweat standing out on his forehead. Too late to draw back now, even if he had wanted to... As though in a dream he saw Mellor's hand drop, and a dull roaring came to his ears. The *Ares* gave a lurch, and Maurice gasped at a sudden feeling of pressure, growing gradually greater and greater until he seemed to be crushed hard against the bottom of his couch. Red sparks started to dance in front of his eyes, and he fought to hold on to his senses. 'Readings!' barked Mellor, and Maurice forced himself to think calmly, despite the painful pressure that seemed to squeeze every scrap of breath from his body. He managed to reply; still the pain grew, until he wanted to shout with the agony of it. Again Mellor called; again Maurice answered. How long could this last? There was a roaring in his ears now that was not due only to the scream of the motors; a third time he gasped out the instrument readings, and then, for a brief moment, the pressure relaxed, and the three of them shot upwards, restrained only by their straps.

'First stage away!' he heard Bruce call, and then they were shot back into their seats again. Once more the pain built up, until he struggled desperately for breath. He never knew how he managed to stay concentrated during the next few minutes - minutes that seemed like hours; even the centrifuge was nothing to this. He struggled desperately, and gripped the sides of his couch so fiercely that his hands went white - surely this could not keep on forever? For the last time he answered Mellor's call of 'Readings!' and his senses drifted... Then, the roar of the engines suddenly stopped. In a pain-racked haze Maurice breathed deeply in his couch - they were in orbit around the Earth.

CHAPTER 5
LOST IN SPACE!

THE DREADFUL pressure had vanished altogether, and Maurice realized that in its place there was a curious sensation that he could not quite fathom. The roar of the engines had ceased, too, and the interior of the *Ares* seemed deathly quiet.

'Phew!' Maurice tried to sit up, forgetting for the moment that he was fastened tightly down to his couch by the supporting straps. 'Bruce... David! That was one hell of a ride!'

'Nothing we didn't expect,' said Bruce's calm voice. 'We're over the worst of it now. Wow! I feel as though I've been pounded with a steam-hammer!'

Maurice fumbled with his straps, and then looked sharply towards the instrument panels. 'Did I... did I let you down? I kept going as long as I could...'

'Frankly,' said Mellor, 'I think you did extremely well. You gave me all the readings of velocity and orientation I asked for, and by the time you became wacked I was pretty well knocked myself. Thankfully we won't have to go through that again. We've broken free from the Earth's pull, and we're out in space in orbit. Apart from the Trans-Martian Injection Burn and minor course alterations, we shouldn't have to use our rocket engines again until we're preparing to land on Mars. That won't be for several months yet, so we'll have plenty of time to recover.' He grinned. 'Careful how you move about. We're weightless now, remember, and it's going to take you a good deal of getting used to.'

Maurice pulled the hinged control panel towards him, as the CAPCOM from Woomera came through with '*Ares*, this is Woomera. Congratulations upon a successful lift-off.' There followed the familiar 'bleep' as their transmission stopped. Maurice acknowledged with 'Woomera, this is *Ares*. Thank you, the Earth looks good from here and I'm even lighter now than I was fifteen minutes ago!'

Maurice looked inquiringly at Mellor as he told him, 'Tell them we'll call up regularly every two hours as per the flight plan. We can keep that up all through the fight, if necessary; it may be as well to keep to the duty rota - I don't suppose any of us feels much like sleeping yet awhile!'

Maurice spoke into his mic, waited for the reply, and then removed his headset. Now that the strain of blasting-off was over, reaction had set in. He felt thoroughly limp, and his chest and ribs still seemed sore and bruised from the crushing pressure he had experienced.

'Well,' said Mellor, after a pause, 'we may as well get busy. Stay where you are for a moment, Maurice. Watch what I do, and make sure you don't make any violent movements once you've unstrapped yourself. I don't want to start the journey by bandaging a broken wrist and ankle, and you'll have to be extremely careful until you get properly used to being weightless.'

Cautiously Mellor unstrapped himself, and then pushed himself gently upwards from the couch. Although he knew what to expect, Maurice could not keep back a cry of amazement. Instead of dropping back on to the springs, Mellor kept on rising - slowly but surely, until he was hovering almost by the 'roof' of the space-ship. Then he seized hold of the central pillar and turned himself slowly over, until he was looking straight down at them, apparently suspended in the air.

'Queer,' he said, thoughtfully. 'You know, I can't help being pleasantly surprised again. I thought I'd be bound to feel sick and giddy to begin with, but I don't - which is a good sign. All right, you two. Un-strap.'

Bruce and Maurice obeyed. Maurice, at least, felt rather uneasy. He had not forgotten his unpleasant experiences in the Woomera gravity chamber, and as the last strap became loose he lay back stiffly as Bruce followed Mellor towards the roof. Then he breathed hard, and pushed away. At once he shot 'upwards' - much more violently than he had expected, and before he realized what was happening he had thudded against the far wall with a jolt that made him cry out.

'Careful, you idiot!' snapped Mellor. 'Why don't you listen to what I said? Your muscles are as strong here as they are on Earth, and if you'd had time to put out your hand you might easily have broken your wrist. Have a little sense!'

Maurice panted, and tried to straighten up. To his amazement, he found that he was 'standing' outwards from the wall, at right angles to the others but with his head close to Bruce's; and he gulped, trying to fight down a feeling of sickness. Instinctively he closed his eyes, and swallowed hard. Bruce's firm hand fell on his shoulder. 'Take it easy, pal. You'll get used to it in a minute or two.'

Maurice forced his eyes open, and managed to grin. 'Talk about a Crazy House!' he said, and gripped the central pillar, pressing himself hard against it until he was standing the same way 'up' as Bruce and Mellor. 'If you hang downwards on Earth, the blood rushes to your head. Why won't that happen up here?'

'Simply because your blood doesn't weigh anything,' said Bruce calmly. 'The human heart works like a pump, and isn't affected by gravity at all, so you needn't worry. You were told all that, don't you remember? Use your brain and concentrate - it'll help

you overcome the sickness. And - we have a solution...
He thrust himself gingerly towards the 'floor', and
opened one of the snugly fitting cupboards. 'Put on
your magnetic boots. The iron strips across the floor
will anchor them down. Actually we'd meant to make
the whole floor iron, but we replaced most of the strips
at the last moment in order to save weight. Here you
are.'

Clumsily, Maurice fitted on the strange metal boots,
and eased himself on to the lower part of the rocket. At
once he felt a slight but perceptible tug, and his feeling
of balance returned as his feet clattered against the
magnetic strip. He still felt strange, since although his
feet were lightly anchored the rest of his body was still
weightless; when he lifted an arm there was no
inclination to drop it, and he felt as helpless as a spider
that has lost its web. Still, the sensation of sickness was
passing. Bruce and Mellor followed, and Bruce gave a
grunt of relief.

'That's better,' he said. 'Thank goodness we
decided to risk keeping some of the iron strips. OK, I
guess we should do the after-launch flight checks?'

Mellor shrugged. 'If anything has gone wrong I
don't see that there's a lot we can do about it, but we
may as well check what we can. You see to the main
computer units, and I'll run the diagnostics on the
software.' He looked quickly at Maurice. 'You look a
bit ill; better strap down for a few minutes, and get over

it. Don't worry. The effect of giddiness will pass off in an hour or two.'

Rather thankfully, Maurice obeyed, and watched as his two companions carried out a careful and systematic check of the circuits and main panel in association with the main Control Centre at Woomera. Somehow, he felt remarkably confident. It was clear that Mellor was brilliant in his own field, even though few people could have looked less like a professor if they tried; and Bruce, too, was obviously immensely competent. For perhaps twenty minutes nothing more was said, but suddenly Mellor looked up, and gave a sharp exclamation. 'Oh-oh,' he said. 'Bruce. Look at this.'

Bruce thrust himself over to the main pillar. 'What?'

'The distance display,' muttered Mellor. 'According to the flight plan and my calculations, we must be something like eight hundred miles from the Earth, but the display shows 'infinity'. You realize what that means?'

Bruce's lips tightened. 'Broken.'

'Quite so. Blast. Why? It was given a thorough systems check before we left and was fine.'

Bruce shrugged. 'It must have got hotter than we expected as we whipped through the lower atmosphere. Well, that's one bit of equipment we can't do without. Unless our telemetry radar is working perfectly, we shan't have a hope in a thousand of making a faultless landing on Mars, and we can only have one shot at it. If we use up too much power, we'll never be able to lift off again with six aboard.'

Maurice broke in, his heart thumping. 'What... what's gone wrong? Is it serious? We seem to be all right...'

'At the moment, we're perfectly all right,' said Mellor grimly, 'but how long we'll stay so is another matter. The trouble is that unless our main radar registers are functioning, we shall be unable to check our distance and position well enough for an accurate Trans-Martian Injection burn or navigating to Mars, let alone for the landing manœuvre. Damn! We couldn't allow for this. Well, there's only one answer. We'll have to do an EVA.'

Maurice blinked. 'Outside? You mean go outside the space-ship?'

'Of course I do,' snapped Mellor impatiently. 'We're well beyond the top of the atmosphere now, so there's no danger of drifting away. We'll leave it for a few minutes yet just in case it rights itself, but I doubt whether it will. If the whole outer casing of the radar installation has been melted by the friction, we shall just have to replace the unit.'

Bruce nodded, and returned to his own checking. Again there was a long silence, and Maurice forced himself to be calm. He knew more or less where the trouble lay. As Lindsell had told him during his lessons in astronautics, landing upon a planet depended entirely upon instruments; unless the crew knew their exact distance and range, the computer would be unable to bring the rocket engines into play at just the right moment, and there could be no second chance. Sections of the radar equipment had to be fitted on to the outer hull of the *Ares*, and if these had been badly damaged during lift-off the astronauts were likely to be left more helpless than an owl in brilliant sunlight.

'Well,' said Mellor at last, 'that's that. Apart from the radar computer, everything is working perfectly. We'd better make up our minds to tackle it straight away; no sense in keeping ourselves on tenterhooks - and we have the TMI burn in 3 hours. Bruce, you'd better go out - this is your speciality and I'll keep a watch here on the panels.'

Maurice's tongue felt dry. 'Shall I come with you?'

Bruce looked at him sharply. 'Do you feel up to it yet? It'll be an experience, you know.'

'I don't care,' said Maurice, with more confidence than he felt, and managed to force a grin. 'After all, there's plenty of room to be sick in space!'

Mellor burst into a laugh. 'You've plenty of guts, anyhow,' he said. 'All right; out you go. Don't be longer than you need, and whatever you do don't look straight at the sun. Now that we're beyond the air, we're wide open to all the short-wave radiations it sends out, and even our space-suit visors aren't perfect. Get busy.'

Maurice levered himself up, and reached for one of the clumsy-looking space-suits that were stored at the foot of the pillar. He had worn them before, during his practices in the gravity chamber, and he knew how they worked. He also knew that they were far from comfortable. The old idea of a space-man's clothing, a thin suit rather on the lines of a diver's rubber suit and with completely flexible arm and leg joints, had proved to be very wide of the mark. A true space-suit was much more in the nature of a rigid starched overcoat, with the joints almost mechanically stiff, heavily-gloved hands, and a helmet which gave a restricted field of view. Silently he climbed into the suit, and followed Bruce into the first of the air-locks.

Bruce shut the inner door, and fastened it securely. 'Sure you feel all right to come?'

Maurice nodded. 'I'm ready.'

Bruce turned the handle that controlled the air supply, and made a quick inspection of Maurice's helmet. The atmosphere hissed out of the air-lock, drawn back into the main body of the *Ares* by powerful pumps, and within perhaps half a minute the indicator registered 'vacuum'. Maurice drew a deep breath. Now that there was no air outside him, he was entirely dependent upon the oxygen supply carried in his suit; nor could he hear anything, except by using his helmet radio. Sound, as he knew, was carried by atmosphere, and where there was no atmosphere there could be no natural sound.

Bruce opened the outer door, and Maurice followed him into the second of the air-locks. Again the pumps drew away the precious oxygen, and Bruce unwound the long, tough cord fastened to his suit, motioning Maurice to do the same. 'Fix your cord on to the hook just outside the door,' he said, his voice strange in the headphones in the helmet. 'Once you start moving when we're outside, you'll just keep on drifting. You can always get back by using your space-suit motor as you've been trained, of course; but motors have been known to fail, and if that happened you'd be beyond all hope of rescue, so it's as well to be on the safe side. For goodness' sake, don't get your cord tangled up with mine.'

Maurice fastened his safety cord and tested it to make sure that it was firmly attached, watching as Bruce operated the locks of the door that led straight into outer space. It was a terrifying thought: here they were, eight hundred miles or more in orbit above the Earth, about to step straight into the void with no protection other than a space-suit and a painfully slender-looking rope... He gulped as the door swung gently open, and he craned his head over Bruce's shoulder.

'All right,' said Bruce calmly. 'Here we go. Take it easy; remember, you can't fall - you're in the same orbit as the *Ares* itself. Follow me.'

They fixed their cords. Then Bruce disappeared through the door, and Maurice followed, his heart pounding against his ribs. The opening was only just big enough for him to squeeze through, and instinctively he shut his eyes. When he opened them again, he could not keep back a shout of amazement.

He was 'floating' in space; the body of the *Ares*, only a few feet away, seemed already far distant, its greyish hull glinting in the harsh light. The sky was inky black, spangled with countless stars; to one side he could see the crescent moon, while to the other lay the sun, no longer the friendly yellow disk he was used to but a blazing, dead-white ball, alien and terrible. Below his feet was spread the great globe of the Earth, looking more like a ball than a schoolroom map. It, too, shone with a bluish light, and he could make out the outlines of Asia and Australia, while cloudy streaks spread across the northern regions and the vast expanse of the Pacific Ocean shone with a dull, leaden light. Maurice caught his breath.

'Bruce! It's... it's unbelievable!'

'Quite a sight, isn't it?' said Bruce, cheerfully. 'I've been out in space before, and each time the sight amazes me.' He hauled gently on his cord, and floated over to Maurice's side. 'Look at those snow-caps covering the poles. We'll see the same sort of thing on Mars, when we're near enough, only ours are much thicker.'

Maurice shivered. The Australian continent was clear enough, and he could estimate the position of the desert rocket range with fair accuracy; it was hard to credit that only two hours ago the *Ares* had been standing in the take-off bowl, ready to hurl herself into the depths of the Solar System.

'Well,' said Bruce, after a pause, 'we'd better get to work. We'll have plenty of time to star-gaze once we know for certain whether we're going to be able to make a decent landing or not. Keep your eyes off the sun, and thrust yourself round to the radar section. I shall probably want you to help me with removing the unit.'

He drifted off, and Maurice followed, playing out his cord as carefully as he could. Bruce worked his way round to the 'nose' of the rocket, close to the main observation window, and peered closely at the stubby projections that rose up from the hull. 'I'm darned if I know,' he muttered. 'They look all right from here, and it's pretty difficult to check them when you have to operate from a space-suit instead of using your hands on the ground. I reckon I'd better dismantle the whole unit, and take it inside.' He looked round. 'Come over here, and hang on to the inner section of the circuit boards case. If it unscrews first go, all well and good; if it doesn't, I shall have to use brute force.'

Maurice clamped his gloved hands round the base of the cylinder. Bruce eased himself round until his head almost touched Maurice's, and wrenched softly. There was no response, and he muttered something under his breath.

'No go?' said Maurice, steadily.

'Not yet. Keep gripping,' said Bruce, and wrenched again. This time the cylinder moved slightly; again he wrenched, and gradually the outer part of the tube screwed off, until he was able to pull it clear of the base. Gingerly he disconnected the remaining circuits, and then drew a deep breath of relief. 'Phew! Thank goodness for that,' he said, and gave Maurice a grin. 'I was half afraid the heat had fused the metal, and if that had happened it would have been difficult, to say the least of it. I'm going inside. You can stay here if you like, though. With any luck, this thing won't take more than thirty minutes to replace. How do you feel about it?'

'I'll wait,' said Maurice.

'Right. Remember, don't look at the sun, and give a call every couple of minutes.'

Bruce propelled himself gently back towards the air-lock door, and Maurice relaxed, hovering within easy reach of the *Ares* hull. Now that the first feeling of strangeness had passed, he was beginning to enjoy himself. A week ago, he had been a shy schoolboy, very much alone and out of his element among men; now he had grown up, and even the wildness of space held few terrors for him. Where was England? He stared at the bluish Earth below, and narrowed his eyes. The light fell away towards one side of the globe, marking the approach of night, and Europe was on the far side, so that it could not be seen. Maurice's eyes ranged round. There was the Great Bear, far more brilliant than at home, with the stars steely points instead of gently twinkling lamps; there was the familiar Pole Star - and there, too, was Mars, the Red Planet, still no more than a blood-red speck. Maurice gazed at it, fascinated. Six months from now, the Earth itself would look something like that...

'All right?' said Bruce's voice, in the earphones.

Maurice replied, 'Yes. It really is a fantastic view. How are you doing - what about the radar?'

'We've replaced the broken unit inside it, thank goodness. It wasn't a big job. The friction had put one of the mother boards out of action, but we'd had the sense to bring some spares. I'm coming out again now.'

Maurice waited. Presently he saw Bruce's bulky, space-suited figure emerge from the air-lock, and thrust towards him; then, suddenly, he saw that something was wrong. Bruce had pushed off too violently. Instead of heading for Maurice, he had plunged away almost at right angles, and a sudden shout sounded in the headphones:

'Maurice! Quick - my cord's faulty, it's come loose... Grab me, for Heaven's sake!'

Maurice gasped, and thrust outwards towards the

drifting figure. Swift as he was, he was not quite quick enough. His safety cord tightened, pulling him up with a violent jerk - he had reached the end of its run, and still Bruce was well out of reach, moving further away every second. 'Bruce! Your motor - use your motor!' Maurice panted.

'I didn't bring it!' Bruce's voice was hoarse with terror. 'Like a fool, I didn't bother - I thought my cord was safe. It's my own fault, Maurice. Keep back!'

Maurice fumbled with his gloves. 'All right,' he said crisply. 'I'm coming after you. Steady on.'

'Don't be an idiot!' Bruce choked, and his voice rose. 'We haven't had time to test those suit motors, and anyhow you've never had any practice with them. You'll only kill yourself too. Now that we've blasted off, you and David will have to work the controls on your own.'

Maurice gulped. Would the safety-rope never unfasten? Barely hearing what Bruce was saying, he wrenched the hook loose, and realized that he too was drifting quickly away from the *Ares*. Bruce had vanished - where was he? Maurice gritted his teeth, and fought down his panic.

'Where are you?' he said, evenly. 'Left or right?'

'Left.' Bruce's voice was blurred and distorted now. 'For the last time, kid, go back! You'll never get to me.'

Maurice forced himself round, and shivered as he saw Bruce's figure in the distance, so far away that it looked almost like a toy. He could hear Mellor speaking, too, but he paid no attention. Frantically he operated the controls of his space-suit motor, and felt the vibration as the small but powerful reaction engines came to life. Next moment he was flashing away from the *Ares* in Bruce's wake, fumbling with the controls. Now he had lost Bruce again... No, there he was; what now? His speed was too great; he reversed the switch, and found himself swinging far over to the right.

'Left - and towards the sun,' choked Bruce. 'I can't stop my drift...'

Maurice set his jaw. He was beginning to get the 'feel' of the motors now. Where the *Ares* was, he no longer cared; his one idea was to reach Bruce and drag him back before it was too late. Again he brought the engines to life, and again he overshot. Now Bruce was above him, kicking his legs feebly in an effort to stop himself spinning over and over... Now he was close at hand - and at last, Maurice's hand shot out and fastened on to Bruce's leg.

Bruce half sobbed. 'For the Lord's sake, kid, get back. We're over a mile away now - you'll never do it. It's my own fault. Get back on your own!'

'Both or neither,' said Maurice evenly, and stared at the distant, shining form of the space-craft. Again he opened up the engines, checking and adjusting their speed, until with agonizing slowness the *Ares* started to draw nearer. They could see Mellor now, floating outside the open air-lock with his safety-cord stretched to the limit.

None of the three ever forgot the next ten minutes. Once the motors in Maurice's suit faltered, and his heart leaped; if they failed now, nothing could save him or Bruce from a dreadful, lingering death in the wastes of Earth orbit. Once they heard Mellor call instructions: 'Swing right - gently!' But for the rest, Maurice remembered little. As though in a daze, he realized that the metal hull was close ahead; he felt Mellor's grip on his belt, and then everything went black. The next thing he remembered was a sting in his throat, and Bruce's anxious face peering down at him.

'Suck this,' said Bruce quietly, holding out a queerly-shaped bottle containing some liquid. 'It'll pull you round. Lord! I wouldn't go through that again for all the iridium on the Moon!'

Maurice put his lips to the neck, and sucked up some more of the sharp, bitter-tasting liquid. Then he choked, and spluttered.

'Phew! What... what happened?'

'You passed out,' said Mellor grimly, 'but not before you'd saved the situation in no uncertain manner. Do you realize what would have happened if you hadn't been so quick on the uptake? Once you start drifting in space, remember, you don't stop; you go on, getting farther away every moment. By the time I could have climbed into my suit and come outside, Bruce would have been so far off that I wouldn't have had a hope of getting to him, or even finding him. We've been very lucky.'

'Not lucky, David; plucky,' said Bruce, and put his hand on Maurice's shoulder. 'I won't embarrass you by trying to thank you, Maurice, but you can probably guess how I feel.'

Maurice grinned feebly. He felt content.

CHAPTER 6

THE VIOLET LAYER

FORMERLY, MAURICE had known that his companions regarded him as a boy who was with them only because he was small and light. His rescue of Bruce made a tremendous difference not only to Maurice himself, but to his companions' attitude towards him; now he was accepted on equal terms, and it was only natural that during the next few weeks he should come to know them very well indeed. The more he saw of Mellor, the more he liked him. The astronaut-scientist had a quick temper, and no patience at all with slowness on the uptake, but his irritability never lasted for long, and he was always ready to laugh at himself. Bruce was of different type. He was older than Maurice both in years and in outlook, but their spirits were similar and Maurice found it hard to realize that he had known him for only a short time. For the first time since the tragic death of his parents, he felt that he was no longer alone, and had some kind of family.

'What happened to your people, Maurice?' asked Bruce quietly, some two months after their launch. Needless to say, there was no true day or night in space, where the sun was always shining, and the normal calendar was meaningless, but there was no way of reckoning time other than by terrestrial standards. 'Are they both dead?'

'Yes. They were killed in a crash, and - well, I haven't got any close relations now. I don't know what I'll do when I get back, if I get back, that's to say!'

'Time enough to talk about that later on,' said Bruce. 'I live at Woomera, of course, and I'd like you to stay on and join our group, if you want to... Well, that can wait. We're not back home yet, by a long chalk.' He stood up and walked over to the shielded observation window, his magnetic boots clattering against the iron strips. 'Since our TMI burn we've been on our way for eight Earth weeks, and Mars seems almost as far off as ever. Look at it!'

He pressed the button which opened the metal shutter, and the two peered out at the distant, glowing disk of the Red World, still shining like little more than a very brilliant star. The Earth, too, was almost starlike now. It was difficult to make out even the sprawling outlines of Eurasia and the Americas, and only the sun remained unchanged. They were well and truly 'in the wilds'.

Time passed. So far there had been no trouble in

keeping contact with Woomera, and either Bruce or Maurice had called up every few hours, but always with the same basic message, 'nothing to report'. For their part, they learned that Sir Robert Lanner had given orders for a new *Ares* to be built, in readiness for the third Martian expedition, while Daniels and her team continued their unsuccessful attempts to get in touch with Leslie Yorke. 'We've about stopped hoping,' signalled Hayley one day, when Maurice was at the radio controls. 'Whatever's hit them, it's put their radio out of action for good.' Neither had the astronomers been able to find out anything new.

Three months... Four... Gradually Mars swelled from a tiny disk into a true globe, far outshining any other body in the heavens apart from the sun; now they could start to see the great dark patches that the old astronomers had thought to be seas, but which were now known to be nothing more than dark tracts. They could see the ochre dust-deserts, too, and even some of the strips which had been given the misleading name of 'canals'. Perhaps five months after leaving Woomera, Maurice caught sight of a tiny star like point close to Mars itself and called Mellor's attention to it.

'What's that, sir? It looks like one of the moons.'

'If you call me 'sir' again,' said Mellor, 'I shall have to ask you to open the air-lock and step outside - without your space-suit this time, toughened spaceman though you are! You've been warned.'

'Sorry, David!' Maurice grinned. 'Still, you haven't answered my question. Is that one of Mars' satellites?'

'Yes; it's Deimos, one of Mars' two moons. The other one, Phobos, is even closer in, only about three thousand miles above the surface of the planet.'

'Two moons,' repeated Maurice, thoughtfully. 'Must be pretty bright at night, then, mustn't it?'

'No, not really. They're called 'moons', but really they're nothing more than chunks of rock. Phobos is about twenty miles across, and Deimos even less. Between them, they wouldn't give more than one five-hundredth of the light that our Moon gives to the Earth.' Mellor paused. 'Still, they may be important to us in the long run. They'll make perfect space-stations, once we've learned enough to make the colonization of Mars a practical possibility, and - hopefully - that won't be so long ahead now. See that reddish tract, near the V-shaped dark marking? That's Aeria, where your uncle and the *Hermes* have landed. If all goes well, we'll come down fairly close beside them.'

'I reckon we'll be lucky if we judge it to within a hundred miles,' muttered Bruce.

Mellor shrugged. 'Nearer than that, I hope. Time will tell.'

Five and a half months... Now Mars loomed large in the sky, its dark tracts, ochre deserts and ice-covered polar caps spread out plainly. Communication with Woomera became difficult and uncertain, and on two occasions contact was lost altogether for several days on end. Now and then Mellor and Bruce spent hours using the on-board computers in making calculations, after which a short burst of power from the rocket engines would alter their course slightly, and Maurice started to feel tense. At last, their long journey was nearing its end.

'Better get some rest,' advised Bruce, after Maurice had at last succeeded in exchanging a brief message with Woomera. 'We'll be starting the landing manœuvre in eight hours from now, and it's likely to be the last peaceful sleep you'll get for a long time. We shan't get much rest once we've come down.'

Maurice obeyed, but for some time he could not sleep. The orange face of Mars kept on floating before his eyes. Somewhere down there, his uncle and two other men were watching for the rescuers who had come to them across fifty million miles of space; if, indeed, they knew that the *Ares* had even started out. Suppose they were too late after all? Suppose Yorke's oxygen had given out, so that they would find nothing but a ruined space-craft and three lifeless bodies? Suppose...

Maurice slept. Hours later, he felt Bruce's hand shaking his shoulder, and blinked sleepily up at him. 'Time to get busy,' said Bruce crisply. 'Thirty minutes to go. So far as we can estimate, everything's going according to plan, but the next hour's going to be about the trickiest of the trip.'

Maurice rubbed his eyes. 'Phew! I was well gone, and no mistake.' He yawned, and unfastened his securing straps. 'What's the risk? We blasted away from Earth all right, and I thought that Mars doesn't pull so hard.'

'Gravity has nothing to do with it,' said Mellor, drily. 'It's not a question of plunging straight down like a shooting star. If we did that, we'd strike the atmosphere of Mars at such a speed that we'd turn the *Ares* into a streak of fire.' He glanced at the displays. 'As a matter of fact, I've an idea that the atmosphere itself may have been the cause of Yorke's disaster. Even now we don't know much about it, except that it's mainly carbon dioxide, and it may well be the unknown factor in our calculations.'

Maurice looked puzzled. 'I don't see what you mean.'

'I don't quite see it myself. We know that there's a region in the atmosphere known as the 'Violet Layer', not because it looks violet - it doesn't - but because it blocks out the short-wave radiations emitted by the sun. We haven't been able to find out just what the Layer is, and it seems to roam, but at least it's absolutely different from anything in our own air. I may be an alarmist, and I sincerely hope I am, but we've no choice but to trust to luck. Get ready, both of you. I shall want readings at regular intervals from now on.'

Maurice shook himself wide awake, and settled down on his couch, his instrument console within easy reach and his eyes fixed on the computer display screens. Bruce lay back on the second couch, while Mellor fastened himself securely, his face set and grim.

'One minute,' he said, after what seemed an eternity. 'Range three hundred miles. Readings?'

Bruce and Maurice rapped out answers. Mellor drew a deep breath, and his eyes became fixed upon the engine computers and countdown displays. 'Ten seconds to Decent Burn...'

'Five... Four... Three... Two... One... Now!' he said harshly, and abruptly the nuclear-ion motors came to life with the full shrill whine that they had not heard for months. Maurice gasped as the familiar feeling of pressure built up again, and he fought for breath. Then the force relaxed slightly, and he choked with relief, spluttering as he called out the readings in response to Mellor's request.

'All well so far,' muttered Mellor, against the roar of the engines. The *Ares* lurched, and even above the scream of the motors Maurice could hear a hissing louder than a thousand snakes all rolled into one. He knew what it meant; they had come into the denser layers of the Martian air, so that the ochre desert could be no more than a few thousand feet below them.

Suddenly the *Ares* pitched again, and Mellor let out a shout, clamping his hands on the console. Lurch...

jerk... Maurice swallowed hard, and hung on to his couch like grim death. It felt almost as though the space-craft had been caught in some mighty hurricane that hurled her about like a leaf in a gale. In vain the engines whined and shrilled; the *Ares* was pitching and rolling badly.

'I've had enough of this,' shouted Mellor. 'Switching to manual.'

In vain Mellor battled with the controls - something was badly wrong, and all three of them knew it.

'The Violet Layer!' breathed Bruce, his face white and strained. 'Stick it, David. We can't have far to go...'

Mellor gasped out something in reply, and for the last time the rocket engines roared, striving to bring the *Ares* level. The pressure was upon them still, even if the violent lurching had grown less, and the ominous hissing had died away to a faint purr... Then, abruptly, came a shock more violent than all the rest. Maurice's straps snapped and he was jolted clear of his couch, and for a few seconds the pain was so intense that he almost fainted. When he could think clearly once more, he realized that all sensation of motion had ceased. Hardly daring to breathe, he opened his eyes.

'David! Have we... have we come down?'

Mellor half turned, and Maurice could see the bitter expression on his face.

'In a way,' he said, his voice harsh and cracked.

'We've landed on Mars all right, but unless I'm very much mistaken I've wrecked the *Ares* in doing it. If we can't put matters right, we're finished.'

CHAPTER 7

THE WILDERNESS OF MARS

MELLOR HAD been right, then. Maurice drew in his breath sharply. There was something in this strange Violet Layer that had first wrecked Yorke's ship, and now their own. He did not need reminding of the plight in which they found themselves. So long as the *Ares* was space worthy, Yorke and his crew had had at least a chance of rescue; but they themselves had none. Even though Sir Robert and his colleagues at Woomera were presumably making all haste to build a new craft, they could not possibly have it ready in time.

'I'm sorry,' muttered Mellor, at last. 'I don't pretend to understand just where the trouble was, but I should have done something to prevent this. You've got me to blame.'

'Don't be an idiot, David,' said Bruce curtly. 'You're talking nonsense, and you know it. Whatever's gone wrong, nobody could have done better than you did; it's some unknown quality of the atmosphere of this damned planet.' He loosened his straps, and stood clumsily up. 'Ouf! Seems funny to feel heavy again after six months in space. My legs are like jelly, in spite of all that time on the exercise equipment.'

Maurice released his own straps, but when he tried to stand up he understood what Bruce meant. The force of gravity upon Mars was much less than at home - a ten-foot leap in the air would be nothing unusual - but it was very different from complete weightlessness, and for the moment he felt as though his feet and arms were made of lead. It was strange, too, to realize that 'up' and 'down' really meant something once more.

'Well,' said Mellor wearily, 'that's that. It was a good try, even if it didn't come off. I should die more peacefully if I could find out just what hit us.'

'Who's talking of dying?' interrupted Maurice, stoutly. 'We're not done yet. Even if we did come down with a bang, we may have escaped without much damage. The *Ares* is pretty tough, after all.'

'Not so tough as that, I'm afraid,' said Mellor bitterly. 'There are certain things we can't protect, things like computers, radar and navigation circuits, and without them we're more helpless than a rowing-boat in a gale. The one bright point is that we've come down pretty near where we meant to, so far as I can make out. We're in Aeria, and if Yorke gave us his position correctly the *Hermes*, or what's left of it, ought to be less than a hundred miles away.'

Bruce clapped him on the shoulder. 'Cheer up, Dave. Remember, we don't know yet how badly the *Hermes* is damaged. It's quite possible that between the bits of both ships, we may be able to patch one of them up enough to take us home. Don't be such a pessimist.'

Mellor squared his shoulders, and gave a mirthless grin. 'Sorry. It's not like me to be like this, but well; I feel I've failed you both when you'd put your trust in me. You're right, of course,' he added, more in his usual manner. 'As soon as we've made a few preliminary checks, we'll try to find out just how bad the damage is. It's just about sunrise on this part of Mars, which gives us a good twelve hours of daylight.'

Maurice nodded, and reached for his space-suit. He remembered that the days on Mars were only a little longer than those of the Earth - unlike those on the Moon, which lasted for over a terrestrial fortnight. The space-suits seemed much more clumsy now than when they had been out in space, where they had weighed nothing, and once inside his suit he found it difficult to move with any freedom. They descended to the second section of the space-craft, ready for their exit through the lower air-locks, down on to the Red Planet.

'Make sure of your oxygen,' said Mellor curtly. 'We've had quite enough mishaps, one way and another, and we don't want any more.'

Maurice obediently checked his air supply, and found it sufficient to last him for twenty-four hours if need be. Bruce was already in the outer air-lock; Mellor followed, and finally Maurice squeezed in, waiting impatiently as Bruce switched on the air-pumps that sucked the oxygen back into the hull of the *Ares*. A few moments more, and the three stepped cautiously from the outer door for their first view of the wild, inhospitable planet to which they had come.

It was not in the least what Maurice had expected. There were mountains in the distance, and there were craters both on the ochre deserts and on the dark areas once thought to be seas, but later found to be mere rock with the occasional clump of what - incorrectly - had been hoped might be a primitive form of moss. Yet even so, somehow or other he still half anticipated seeing a network of watery channels, perhaps with green stuff growing nearby, and with oases here and there. Actually, nothing of the kind could be seen. In the far distance, several miles away, there were some low hills, but otherwise the scene was featureless. To every side stretched the reddish-ochre plain, unrelieved by the slightest trace of life, and somehow utterly unfriendly. Maurice gasped.

'Phew!' he said, softly. 'What a place!'

'Not exactly a hive of activity, is it?' said Mellor, in his usual dry tone. 'Wouldn't it be nice if we were met by a party of Martians shouting 'Welcome!' and rolling out red carpets for us.' He paused, and then continued, 'I wonder what will happen here during the next few centuries?'

Bruce shrugged. 'Plenty, I expect. There'll be domes, and communication centres, and all the usual ancillary support bits and pieces, to say nothing of rocket ports and roads. Pity we shan't be here to see it. There's plenty of red carpet, at least!' He stooped down, and picked up some of the dusty material with his gloved hand. 'Iron oxide-rust, I presume?'

'Not rust,' said Mellor slowly, peering downwards at the reddish grains. 'Years ago, a French astronomer named Dollfus suggested that Mars might be covered with a layer of a mineral known as limonite, spread about in a pulverized state. He was right - the probes proved that. It's rather like red sand.'

Maurice had turned away, and was staring upward. Even here everything was unfamiliar. The sky was not blue; it was yellowish pink, with a tinge of mauve down at the horizon. He pointed to the west, or where he judged the west to be, 'Look there, David. Is that the Violet Layer you've been talking about?'

'Of course it isn't,' said Mellor impatiently. 'The sky's pink because there isn't enough air to make it blue, but there is dust in it, and that causes the colour. The Violet Layer - well, goodness knows what it really is. At any rate, we can't see it.'

Bruce grunted. 'It may interest you, but at the moment I wouldn't care if the sky turned out to be pale green with purple spots. We'll have plenty of time to admire the scenery once we've fixed up the *Ares*, and the sooner we start the better. Besides, we've got to think about finding Yorke and the others. Is there any point in trying to call them up by radio, do you think?'

'I doubt it; we couldn't reach them as we were approaching Mars. But we may as well try,' said Mellor. 'I imagine that the atmosphere of this infernal planet has a reflecting layer, which will at least make it possible to keep radio touch beyond the distance of the horizon, and there's always a chance that the radio in the *Hermes* is still effective over short distances. That's your job, Maurice. You know the frequencies. See what you can do, while we start checking the damage.'

Rather reluctantly Maurice clambered back into the air-lock, switched on the pumps that flooded it with air, and removed his space-suit. He returned to the crew cabin; somehow, he was no longer frightened. Even if the *Ares* was in need of major repairs, he had confidence in Mellor and Bruce, and it was good to feel that he was at least somewhere near the uncle he had never met. Eagerly he tuned the transmitter, switched to full power, and called:

'Hello, *Hermes*. Space-ship *Ares* calling the crew of *Hermes*. We have landed in Aeria. Can you hear us? Over.'

Breathing hard, he waited for a reply. None came; and again he called, this time using Morse, praying that he would hear answering 'dot-dashes' in his headset.

Once again he was disappointed, and his heart sank. It might be that something in the Martian atmosphere, perhaps the deadly Violet Layer, prevented his signals from being heard; it might be that Yorke's radio had failed completely, so that even if he could hear he could not send; but it might also mean that there were no living men left to hear. It was six months now since he had stood in the radio room at Woomera and listened to his uncle's one brief, unfinished message, and much could have happened in that time.

Struck by a sudden thought, he reached for the map of Mars that lay on the chart-table. On it Mellor had marked their estimated position - latitude 5° north, longitude 320° - on the desert between the dark tracts of Deltaton Sinus and Sinus Sabæus, and he added it to his message. Looking for Yorke would be a difficult business with almost the whole of Aeria to choose from, as he well knew, and if the crew of the stranded space-ship could in fact receive radio messages it would be far easier for Yorke to find the *Ares*.

Again and again he called, but there was no response apart from the subdued crackle of solar and cosmic noise, and Maurice's spirits sank lower and lower. He had hardly realized until now how anxious he was to meet the uncle who was his only surviving relative if indeed Leslie Yorke did still survive. He looked at his watch, and saw that he had been sitting at the radio set for a full two hours. Glumly he carried on, sending messages at intervals of perhaps two minutes, but always with the same lack of success.

'No luck?' said a voice at last, and he realized that Bruce was standing beside him, minus space-suit, and looking white and drawn. 'I might have guessed it. Everything's going wrong on this blasted trip. I reckon we ought to have been due for a bit of good luck, for a change.'

Maurice whipped off his earpiece. 'What's the verdict, Bruce? Can we lift off again, or can't we?'

Bruce laid a hand on his shoulder. 'Take it easy, pal. It's bad news, I'm afraid.'

Maurice tensed. 'Well?'

'We could blast off, all right,' said Bruce slowly, 'but it wouldn't do us much good. You see, the navigation unit has really gone now - smashed to pieces. That last jolt was too much; it must either have hit something solid as we came down, or just disintegrated because of the sheer force of the decent and landing. Anyhow, the boards are useless. Without them, we couldn't control the *Ares* any more than a blind man could find his way across the Sahara. We'd have no chance of getting near the Earth, even, and if by a miracle we did get within range we'd never be able to land. We'd just go on drifting and drifting through the Solar System until our food and air gave out, and we died like rats in a trap.'

Maurice said nothing. The disaster was so complete that for a moment he was unable to understand just what it meant. Unless they could find the *Hermes*, then, they had no chance - it was a choice of dying on Mars, or dying somewhere out in space...

'Haven't we any spare units with us?'

'We used up some of our spares soon after we blasted off, remember; I'm not likely to forget that little affair.' Bruce grinned, but there was no humour in it. 'Unfortunately, it's not a question of simply repairing an isolated unit. This time the whole installation is smashed - it looks as though it had been put on a steel plate and hammered to bits. No, I'm afraid we've got to face it. We're in a pretty nasty jam.'

'That's rather a mild way of putting it,' said Mellor, pushing open the door of the inner air-lock and throwing his space-suit down on the floor. 'If we ever come through this, and I have another chance of coming here, I'm going to bring at least half a dozen spare navigation and control circuit boards. It was madness not to wait the few extra days until we'd had time to get some ready, but we couldn't foresee this sort of thing. I take it you've had nothing from the radio?'

'Not a squeak,' said Maurice wearily. 'Either they're dead, or they can't hear us, or they can't answer us. I've sent our position fifty times at least, but I don't suppose for a moment that they've picked it up. If only we knew just where they were!'

Mellor looked at the map, and made a quick calculation. 'If the position they sent us was the right one, they're about ninety to ninety-five miles north west of us. Under Martian gravity conditions, that would take us, well, about sixteen hours' walking time; say twenty to be safe. Add another twenty for the trip back, and fifty for searching, and we'd have to be away the best part of four days. It'd be tight going, without renewing our oxygen from the main supply.'

'We can carry enough for a couple of hundred hours,' began Bruce.

'I know, but you've got to remember that once we're out of sight of the *Ares* it won't be easy to find it again. The horizon's much closer than that of the Earth, because Mars is smaller and has a more sharply curved surface. Also, there are no landmarks to go by - apart from those hills in the distance, and I expect one hill on Mars looks very like another. And the other bad news is that the radar homing beacon - being part of the navigation unit - isn't working either, so we'll have nothing to home in on and guide us back.'

'Compass?' suggested Maurice.

'Mars' magnetic field is very unreliable...' Mellor paused, and stared at the instrument panel. 'That's queer. Look at that needle, Bruce. Has it jammed?'

Bruce tapped the complicated direction-indicator, and raised his eyebrows. 'Seems all right, but well, hang it, it can't be. The needle's pointing upwards, or darned near it.'

'So I can see,' said Mellor quietly. 'Well, well! We

live and learn. You realize what it means?'

Maurice hesitated. 'No. What?'

'The Violet Layer. I don't know how or why, but I'm ready to bet my last penny that the infernal thing is intensely magnetic. If so, it would account for the buffeting we got, the failure of the instruments, and everything else. Amazing! A roaming, magnetised area of atmosphere.'

Bruce shrugged helplessly. 'Who on earth heard of a movable magnetic pole thousands of feet up in the air?'

'Nobody, but we're not on Earth, remember. We're on Mars, which is a very different thing. But it does explain why a number of the earlier Mars probes crashed and malfunctioned inexplicably.' Mellor glared at the compass as though it were deliberately misleading him, and gave it an irritable tap. 'Well, I suppose it doesn't make much difference now, except that we shall have to be doubly careful if and when we blast off again. At any rate, it'll be no use relying on compass bearings to guide us across this confounded desert. The only answer will be to use the sun and the stars, which won't be particularly accurate, to say the least.'

'You mean to have a go at finding the *Hermes* then?'

'What else? I certainly don't propose to sit here for the next nine months and wait for our air to run out,' said Mellor, impatiently. 'Even if the new *Ares* could be made ready in time, the same thing would happen again, and by the time we'd finished we'd have a whole fleet of crashed space-ships on Aeria each trying to rescue the other. We'll try and call up Woomera, needless to say, and tell them, but I think we'll find that the Violet Layer, as it's above us, is quite strong enough to blank out all radio waves completely.'

'Uncle Leslie got through once,' said Maurice, thoughtfully.

'I know, but I think he was decidedly lucky. One of the few things astronomers have found out about the Layer is that there are times when it clears away, for some reason that we can't understand, and leaves the surface open to the full blast of the short-wave radiations sent out by the sun. Perhaps that's how and when Yorke got through. But for all we know the Layer might not clear again, possibly for years. I seem to remember that there was a wide clearing of the Layer just before the message came through. It only lasted for about half an hour, though. Incidentally,' he added soberly, 'I'm mightily relieved that we didn't have any problems from solar radiation all the time we were on our way here. Some people believed that we would.'

There was a long silence. All three were thinking furiously to work out some way of escaping from the trap into which they had fallen, but it was only too painfully clear that the situation could hardly be worse. Food was no problem, but water would have to be strictly rationed - unless they could find some extra supply on Mars itself, which was highly unlikely as they were far from the polar regions - and their oxygen could hardly last them for more than twelve months. After that, they would die slowly and terribly from suffocation. Yet what was the alternative? If they hurled themselves back into space, they would die just as surely. Without the sensitive radar 'eyes', their chances of reaching home were hopelessly slim.

'Well,' said Mellor at last, 'we shall have to work out some plan of action. It's obvious that some of us, at least, will have to take the chance and strike out across the desert. The point is, shall we keep together or not?'

Maurice could not help giving a shiver. The idea of being left alone on this wild, desolate world was not a pleasant one. 'I'm all for sticking together. There's a certain amount of safety in numbers.'

Bruce shrugged. 'Why? We're hardly likely to find any dangerous life-forms; apart from the crew of the *Hermes*, there can't be a living thing within fifty million miles of us. Still, I'm rather inclined to agree with you. I don't fancy being on my own.'

'Strictly speaking,' said Mellor, 'we ought to split up, in fact we'll have to, little as I look forward to it. The only possible course is to make our way towards the position Yorke gave us, and when we're close to it spread out and comb the area as thoroughly as we can. It'll take time, and we'll have to chance our portable oxygen supplies seeing us through, but there's no alternative. On the other hand I think we'll leave it until after tonight.'

'Why? If we're going to do it at all, let's start,' said Maurice, and shook himself. 'Gosh! It's not going to be funny.'

Mellor paused. 'I've been thinking things over,' he said slowly. 'The more I puzzle my brains about that damned Violet Layer, the more baffled I am. It simply doesn't make sense, but it exists, and we can't deny it. I'm wondering whether nightfall will make any difference to it. The reflecting layers in the Earth's atmosphere are affected by sunlight, and it's just within the bounds of possibility that Yorke might manage to call us up after dark - always provided that his transmitter isn't completely out of action.'

'I see,' muttered Bruce. 'It's a long shot, but in a position like this anything's worth trying. How long shall we have to wait?'

'Well, the sun must have risen here about an hour ago, which means that it'll set again in about eleven hours from now. For a spell, around early afternoon, you could even go for a stroll, if you feel like having another look at the scenery.' Mellor gave a mirthless grin. 'Otherwise, I'm afraid there is precious little we can do. Trying to patch up the navigation system is so utterly out of the question that I'm probably not even going to attempt it, so I'll amuse myself by carrying out a thorough check of the main engine systems motors and computer circuits just in case we ever have the chance to use them again.'

The hours seemed to drag. Maurice seated himself at the communications console, and made vain attempts to call up first the *Hermes* and then Woomera; but no replies entered into his headset, and as the sun rose higher in the Martian sky the background crackling became so loud that his head reeled and he had to turn the volume right down. Evidently Mellor was right when he said that the solar rays affected the mysterious, deadly Layer that had brought disaster to the *Ares*. At last conditions became so bad that he gave up in disgust, and switched the radio computer off. 'No go,' he said, wearily. 'It's like trying to hear a pin drop when there's a rock band playing. I reckon it's hopeless to try again before the sun sets. What's the time, Bruce? Martian time, I mean?'

'About mid-day,' said Bruce, looking up from the computer circuits he was checking. 'David, do you think there's any harm in our taking a walk over to those mountains? We've got three or four hours, and it shouldn't take long to get there. I suppose there's always a chance of our finding something interesting.'

Mellor grunted. 'All you're likely to find is dust, dust, and yet more dust. Still, there's no reason why you shouldn't have a look round; we may as well find out as much as we can, particularly if there's any prospect of sending a report back to Earth before we die. Don't run any risks. I'll give you an hour and a half, but no more.'

'You're not coming?'

'I am not. I'm likely to have quite enough of the Martian landscape before I'm through, and I much prefer to stay here and finish checking the control systems. Keep in touch by radio, if you can.'

Maurice well remembered seeing an old science fiction film in which travellers to Mars could walk around in the daytime without full space-suits. Unfortunately, things had not turned out that way, and full suits were needed all the time; they were stiff and uncomfortable, and even though they were fully insulated it was unwise to use them for extended periods under conditions of extreme heat and cold. The face-pieces were transparent, but the back-packs containing the oxygen supply were unpleasantly bulky.

Bruce and Maurice connected up oxygen sufficient for sixteen hours' supply, and checked the suits to make sure that nothing was wrong. To run short when well away from the *Ares* would be fatal.

'How far dare we go?' asked Maurice, as he finished checking.

'Not too far.' Mellor looked out over the landscape. 'I don't for a moment think that you will find anything of the slightest use, but I suppose one never knows. Keep in touch.'

CHAPTER 8

THE DUST-STORM

MAURICE FELT quite eager as he followed Bruce out of the air-locks, despite their desperate situation. After all, he was going to explore a strange world, and only three Earthmen had ever landed on Mars before them. Even if it was generally believed that the whole planet was lifeless, one never knew... He dropped lightly on to the dusty ground, and pointed towards the distant mountain range. 'Over there?' he said, his voice sounding thin and small in the earpieces. 'They can't be more than a mile or two off.'

Bruce shrugged. 'It's a bit difficult to judge. The atmosphere's much clearer than ours, but of course the horizon is much closer. I think they're more like three miles away than two, but we'll soon see. Come on.'

He set off at a brisk pace, and Maurice followed. 'Walking' on Mars was very different to walking on Earth; the gravitational pull was reduced by two thirds, and all movements seemed to be in slow motion. Once

Maurice jumped upwards with all his strength, and cried out as he found himself with his feet high above Bruce's head. For a moment he felt alarmed, and then realized that he was dropping so gently that he landed with no more of a jar than if he had stepped off a two-foot bank on Earth.

'Steady on,' said Bruce, and chuckled. 'The more you leap about the more oxygen you'll use, and I'll bet we're going to need every scrap of it before we're through. I'd cut out the gymnastics, if I were you. Hello... look there.'

Maurice strained his eyes. 'Where?'

'Dead ahead, between those two peaks. It looks like a dark green patch. Can you see it?'

'I can see something,' muttered Maurice, after a pause. 'Plants, do you think?'

'Plants? Hardly. We'll go and see, anyhow. I wish we'd had the sense to bring binoculars.'

A thought struck Maurice. 'We haven't brought any weapons, either. Suppose... suppose we do meet some sort of life?'

Bruce laughed out loud. 'You've been reading too much science fiction. The only life you're likely to meet here is three men, and you won't need a gun or a rifle to deal with them!' He switched on his radio, and pulled his visor down over his face. 'Hello, David. Receiving me?'

The earphones crackled. 'Yes. What is it?'

'We don't know, but there's some sort of dark patch at the bottom of one of those mountains. We're going to have a look.'

'Give it my love,' said Mellor drily. 'If you do find any green men, you'd better bring one back with you; they may tell us something of interest, though I doubt it. Out.'

For perhaps twenty minutes Bruce and Maurice walked on, until the *Ares* had become a tiny speck in the distance and the mountains loomed ahead. Now and then Maurice glanced anxiously towards the sun. It was almost overhead now, shining down with a strong, whitish light and throwing their shadows on to the dusty plain. He could see too that it looked much smaller than the sun he was used to, and somehow the light was eerie, not unlike very powerful moonlight. Although the sky remained that curious dark pinkish colour, he could see no stars; nor could he glimpse either of Mars' two tiny moons.

The mountains themselves were comparatively low, and sloped gently up from the level plain in a way that reminded him of sand hills. Now that they were nearer, the dark patch had become more obvious, and presently he could see that it was distinctly greenish in colour, contrasting sharply with the reddish-ochre of the desert and the mountains. Instead of being an isolated spot, it looked as though it were the beginning of a strip that led back through a valley between the hills.

'What do you make of it?' he asked, at last.

'Same as you,' said Bruce briefly. 'In other words, nothing - except that it's some kind of different surface dust. How long have we been gone?'

'Only half an hour. No need to hurry back yet.'

Bruce made no reply, and the two made their way across the barren, monotonous desert until they were close to the dark patch. As they had expected, it was just some kind of greenish dust mineral deposit - not moss or bushes or trees. Bruce walked over to the nearest patch, bent down and lifted some up.

'Funny stuff,' he commented, letting it fall. 'I wish we could take some back to Earth - the geologists would be fascinated. It seems to lie just on top of the red felsites. I suppose it picks up a certain amount of wetness from the air.'

'Rain?'

'Of course not, you idiot. I don't suppose its rained anywhere on Mars for the last million years at least. But when the spring comes, the ice caps at the poles melt, and the winds must bring some of the wet as far as the equator. After all, our own cactus plants can live under conditions that aren't so very different with regard to moisture.' He paused, and stared ahead at the greenish strip that ran along the valley. 'I'd like to have a look on the other side of those hills. Do you reckon we can chance it?'

'Why not?' said Maurice. 'We've only been

walking for about forty minutes, and our oxygen will last for a good many hours yet.'

'I wasn't thinking about oxygen, I was thinking about the sun. It's well past noon now, and the temperature drops pretty quickly in the afternoon. Bruce stared up at the sky. 'We'll carry on for a bit, but if we don't come across anything interesting we'll turn back.'

The mountains were rather higher than they had looked, perhaps because the slope up from the plain was so gentle. Like the desert, they were coated with the reddish-ochre deposit, and their tops were rounded instead of sharp and jagged. So far as could be seen, the greenish mineral was only in the valley, and did not extend far up the sides of the hills. The valley itself sloped upwards, and perhaps half a mile ahead was a low bank that hid the view beyond. Bruce and Maurice wasted no time; they set off again, but before they reached the crest of the bank Maurice paused, and stared upwards.

'What's wrong?' said Bruce quickly, turning.

'I... I don't know what it was,' muttered Maurice, and pointed. 'Look there. Can you see anything?'

Bruce squinted. 'Not even a cloud. Why?'

'I thought I caught sight of... of something flying,' said Maurice slowly. 'It may have been imagination, but I don't think so. It looked almost like some kind of huge bird.'

Bruce set his lips. 'Steady on, pal. Don't forget that the air's thin enough even down here, and no bird could possibly live at much above a thousand feet, even if there was anything to live on. Don't let your mind play tricks.'

Maurice shook his head. 'It's not that. There was something up there; I'm positive of it.' He thought for a while. 'It might have been a shooting-star, I suppose.'

Bruce swept the sky with his keen eyes. 'You wouldn't be likely to see a shooting-star in broad daylight. This so-called sunshine is queer stuff, though; it may affect our eyes, and that's probably the answer. I simply won't believe in Martian birds.' He grinned suddenly. 'If we meet a few camels and ostriches as well, I'll apologize! Incidentally, isn't it about time we called up the *Ares*?'

Maurice nodded. 'Hello, David. Hello, David. We're just going over the top of the ridge. Over.'

There was no reply, and Maurice frowned. The background crackling had grown louder, but Mellor's voice could not be heard; and again he called, wondering what had gone wrong.

'No luck, eh?' said Bruce, thoughtfully. 'Try some Morse, then. He's bound to be listening out.'

Maurice tapped the small Morse key built into the communications unit on the left arm of his space-suit, but still there was no answer, and he gave a grunt of annoyance. 'Damn it all. The hissing's a lot louder - do you think it's that infernal Violet Layer again?'

'I expect so,' said Bruce soberly. 'We've a lot to blame it for already. Well, what do we do? Go back?'

Maurice hesitated. 'I don't see why. After all, the *Ares* is still within sight, and nothing can have happened. It seems stupid to go back without having a look across the hills now that we've come this far.'

'All right,' said Bruce. 'Let's get going, then. I don't suppose for a moment we'll see anything more interesting than another stretch of desert, but it can't do any harm.'

Maurice gave up on his radio efforts, and the two picked their way along by the side of the greenish strip until they could see over the top of the bank. The sight that met their eyes was unexpected, to say the least of it. Instead of a flat, featureless plain like the one they had left, the whole desert seemed to be dotted with patches of darkness, while some way over to the south they could see a well-marked line that looked like a deep crack. Behind them, the hills cut off their view of the *Ares*; ahead, they could make out a range of banks that gave the impression of dust heaped up by the wind.

Maurice drew a deep breath. 'Wow! I didn't bargain for this. Do you suppose that crack's one of the canals we've all heard so much about?'

Bruce shrugged helplessly. 'Hardly. But I must say I'd like to have a closer look at it; there's just a chance we might find a certain amount of water trace. Do you feel up to carrying on for a few minutes more?'

'Still thinking about my bird?' grinned Maurice. 'Don't worry about me - I'm game. Let's go and search round for a few of your ostriches.'

The mineral deposits here were thicker and higher than those on the near side of the hills, even though it rose to a level of only half an inch or so above the dust, and as they approached the canal-like crack, it seemed to become a slightly darker green. Maurice looked around. He was no believer in 'second sight', but he had a sudden feeling that they were walking into danger, and his immediate impulse was to turn back. Had it not been for the affair of the 'bird', he would have said so, but as things were he kept silent until they had reached the very edge of the chasm.

'It's pretty deep,' muttered Bruce, peering down into the shadowed crack. 'I can only just see the bottom. We could climb down easily enough - do you think it's worth it?'

'No. It looks as dry as a bone, and I don't fancy going for a scramble with oxygen packs on my back,' said Maurice bluntly. 'We've been away for longer than we meant, anyway. I reckon we ought to make tracks back to the *Ares*.'

'I suppose you're right,' agreed Bruce rather reluctantly, straightening up and blinking his eyes hard. 'Lord! This light makes my eyes water. I wish these darned suits weren't so uncomfortable. We'd better not waste any more time, or we'll hear a few home truths from David.'

Maurice said nothing, but stood stock still, listening intently. Bruce tapped him sharply on the shoulder.

'Wake up. We'll have to get moving...'

'Quiet,' snapped Maurice softly. 'I can hear something, Bruce. It's a sort of whistling noise - like the wind, only it's miles away. Can you hear it too? Am I dreaming?'

'I can hear it,' said Bruce quietly, after a pause. 'What fools we've been! There is something here, after all - we were raving mad to come this far without weapons...' He seized Maurice's arm, and pointed. 'Over there, by the foot of the hills! What the devil is it?'

Maurice shrank back. A swirling, formless mass had broken away from the side of the hill, and seemed to be making straight for them; the whistling grew louder and shriller, and then suddenly Bruce realized what it was. 'Oh no - it's a dust-storm.' he barked out. 'Of all the infernal luck... Hold on, Maurice this is going to be no joke.'

Maurice wheeled round. 'The crack - quickly,' he shouted. 'I can see a sort of ledge over there, it may protect us from the worst of it. Hurry!'

Grabbing Bruce's arm, he pelted along the side of the gaping chasm until he had almost reached the gentler part of the sloping side. Perhaps twenty feet down, less than a fifth of the complete drop to the bottom, he could see a narrow ledge that would just hold them both, but while they were still some distance away from the ledge the dust-storm caught them. Maurice felt as though he was being shaken by giant hands; he panted desperately, and battled his way along, but he could no longer see more than a few inches in front of his nose, and the screaming of the wind sounded like a thousand demons. He almost fell, and realized dimly that Bruce was beside him.

'We'll have to shelter - or it'll wreck our space-suits,' gasped out Bruce wildly, and staggered as the wind buffeted him mercilessly. 'Now or never!'

Blinded and out of breath, Maurice became aware that he had reached the top of the gentler slope that led down to the ledge, and he paused. In front of him the sides of the chasm seemed to drop with alarming steepness, and even on Mars a fall of something like fifty or seventy-five feet could have only one result, but their only chance was to plunge down and risk gaining a foothold on the ledge. Holding his breath, Maurice fell flat and scrambled his way down, his gloved hands clawing at every bit of rock, and his feet groping for any sort of foothold. At last he kicked against solid rock, and crouched down thankfully. Bruce was not so fortunate. Before he had scrambled more than a few feet, he missed his hold, rolled down the steep gradient and landed with a jolt on his legs that jarred every bone in his body. Had Maurice not hurled himself forward and grabbed his shoulders, nothing could have saved him from falling headlong to the bottom of the chasm.

Maurice panted. 'Bruce! Are you... are you all right?' He had to shout to make his voice audible through the radio above the thin shrilling of the wind, and even down here the dust swirled and tore; the pale white sunlight was blotted out, and they might well have been at the bottom of a coal-mine. 'Bruce!'

Bruce groaned. 'God! My ankle! I think I've broken it or twisted it. If only we could see what we're doing!'

'It can't last long,' muttered Maurice with more confidence than he felt, and steadied Bruce with his arm. 'Once it's over, we can get back into the light.'

'We'll have to,' said Bruce grimly, and then let out a yell of pain. 'If we don't get back to the *Ares* within the next few hours, the oxygen will run out and that'll be the finish. What idiots we've been!'

For what seemed hours the dust whirled around them, and the screaming of the wind reached a new pitch of intensity. Maurice lost all count of time. Deliberately he kept his eyes away from the luminous dial of his watch, and tried to make his mind a blank. He realized suddenly that it was starting to grow horribly dark. Their suits gave them protection, but not enough, and Maurice began to feel cold and numb all over.

'How long?' whispered Bruce, at last.

Maurice stared. 'Two and a quarter hours,' he said, evenly. 'Shall we risk it? I believe the storm's dying down a bit.'

Bruce groaned. 'We'd never manage to scramble up in the dark - it'll take a bit of doing even in broad daylight. Still, we'll have to try it soon, unless we want to stay here for good. Give it another ten minutes.'

Every minute seemed an eternity, but there was no doubt now that the storm had passed its peak. The howling of the wind had died away to little more than a soft whine, and a little light was returning; slowly it increased, and just before Bruce's deadline the two looked up to see that the sky was almost clear. Yet it had changed. In place of the pink colour they had become used to, it was an ugly purple, and both knew only too well what that meant. The sun was sinking, and at any moment now the bitter chill of a Martian afternoon would be upon them.

'Now for it,' said Maurice, and stood wearily up. 'Does your ankle still hurt?'

'It's pretty bad,' admitted Bruce soberly. 'Still, I can do the climb by using my hands to take most of the weight, and once we're on level ground again I'll have to see how fast I can go. Be ready to give me a heave when I need it.'

Now that they could see again, some of the terror had left them; and the climb back to the top of the chasm was not so bad as they had expected, partly because the slope was far from sheer and partly because they could reach out for hand-grips that they had missed on their desperate plunge down. Maurice was first out, and Bruce followed, crawling over the lip of the crack and sprawling facedown on the dusty ground, panting to get his breath back. All traces of the dust-storm had passed now, and the Martian desert was as lonely and calm as it had been when they first saw it, though far in the distance they could still hear a low whine.

'It's getting pretty cold outside,' said Maurice, shivering as he stared at the deep purple horizon and the setting sun. 'Ready?'

He turned to find Bruce kneeling up; his face dead white and twisted with agony, while one of his ankles was bent at an unnatural angle. 'I... I'm afraid not, pal. I've done something to my left ankle - broken it, I think; and the other one's not so good, either. It can't be helped.'

Maurice caught his breath. 'You mean you can't walk?'

'I can't even stand up,' said Bruce, and gasped. 'I knew I'd crocked myself when I landed on that damned ledge, but I didn't know it was as bad as this... Tell David I'm sorry. You two will have to get on without me.'

Maurice stared. 'What do you mean?'

Bruce gave a cracked laugh. 'I should have thought

it was pretty plain. Within a few hours our air will be out and I haven't a hope of getting back. I can't crawl at much more than a mile an hour, and there's no sense in your throwing your life away as well. You'll have to go on by yourself.'

Maurice dropped down, and put his gloved hands to Bruce's ankle. Even through the covering boot he could feel the wrenched bones, and he knew at once that Bruce was really in trouble. He knew a little about first-aid, but it was impossible for him to deal with the injury, and in any case he had nothing that could be used as a splint or bandage.

'Get going,' said Bruce harshly. 'The longer you wait here, the less chance you'll have of saving yourself.'

'I can carry you,' began Maurice.

'Don't be an idiot. I know we don't weigh as much as we do at home, but it's hopeless for you to try to drag me all the way back to the *Ares*. You might manage it if we had three or four hours' grace, but we haven't. It's an order, Maurice - get back!'

Maurice set his jaw. 'Get this into your head, Bruce. I'm not leaving you here, and that's final. It's both or neither. Come on - try to pull yourself up on to my shoulders.'

Bruce half choked, and shook his friend's hand away. 'You crazy fool, Maurice! Have a little sense - there's no other way out. Once you get back to the

other side of the ridge, you may be able to call up David
and get him to come over with more oxygen...'

'No time,' said Maurice briefly, and knelt down.
'Up you get.'

'I won't. There's David to be thought about, as well.
He can't manage on his own, and if you do find the
Hermes and blast off again it'll be easier to take five
than six.'

Maurice shrugged. 'I've told you that it's both or
neither. If you keep on like this, we'll both be here until
we choke. Grip hold of my shoulders, and hoist
yourself up - I can manage all right.'

Bruce groaned, and clasped Maurice's body, heaving
himself into an upright position and easing himself
forward until his full weight was upon the boy's back.
Maurice staggered. He was tough and wiry, but even
under the weakened gravity conditions Bruce felt
horribly heavy, and as he set off across the desert he
wondered muzzily whether his strength would hold out
even as far as the ridge. If only he could make Mellor
hear.

'Keep over to the right,' he heard Bruce say. 'Make
for the valley - the way we came. It's our one hope!'

Maurice had no breath to reply. His heart was
pounding as though it would burst, and water streamed
from his eyes; his head was bent forward so that he
could hardly see more than a few yards in front of him,
and dimly he realized that the darkness was closing in

now. Then he was climbing more steeply; now he had reached the crest of the ridge, and he could hear Bruce calling Mellor, but he could not make out the words. Suddenly he caught his foot and fell forward, pitching Bruce heavily to one side.

Bruce struggled to his knees, his teeth chattering and his face twisted with pain. 'You can't do it, Maurice! We can't have more than a few minutes left. Run for it!'

Maurice panted desperately, and somehow managed to heave Bruce back on to his shoulders. His muscles ached, and every second the deathly chill increased, until despite his space-suit his whole body felt cool. Bruce had stopped calling; he was unable to help, and the shock of the accident had now gripped him, so that his clasp loosened until Maurice had to hold him by sheer force. The sky was almost black now, and the light was failing, but somehow Maurice managed to stagger on, fighting against the wild impulse to collapse upon the ochre desert and lie there until the end came...

He lost track of time, distance, direction - everything. He just had his head down, eyes on the ground in front, and he walked in intense, stubborn effort and concentration. He could not remember where the *Ares* lay, and neither could he pause to reason it out. The only thoughts that hammered into his brain were that he must keep with Bruce, and that he must keep going. It seemed as though the Martian desert stretched for a million miles to every side of him, barren and unfriendly; red and green sparks danced in front of his eyes, and he cried out. Then - was it imagination, or was there someone's hand on his arm, pulling him along? His legs buckled under him; he made a last supreme effort, and then everything went dizzy. Was he still walking or was this blackness the beginning of death? Was he still out in the desert? Maurice panted, and blinked his eyes open.

'All right,' said a firm voice, and Maurice realized that he was back in the familiar cabin, lying full-length on a couch with Mellor bending over him. 'Don't try to get up yet. I've given you a pretty strong injection, and you're bound to feel drowsy.' He straightened up, and gave a twisted smile. 'For sheer courage, young Maurice, I think you take a good deal of beating. It was touch and go.'

Maurice stirred. 'Bruce... is Bruce all right?'

'Yes, thanks to you - apart from a couple of damaged ankles. How the two of you got away with it, I for one shall never know,' said Mellor. 'By sheer luck I happened to pick up a headset when you first called out on your way back, and needless to say I came in search of you. There was no time to get you more oxygen, so I had to do the next best thing and drag you the last few yards on your own. If you'd given in then, it would have been hopeless, but you were actually inside the air-lock before you collapsed.'

Maurice sat slowly up. His head ached violently, and his body felt like one great bruise, but he could think clearly once more; and he grinned feebly, rubbing his eyes. Bruce, lying on the next couch with his ankles swathed in bandages, leant over towards him.

'That's the second time you've risked your neck for me,' he said, quietly. 'I think...'

'Don't,' Maurice interrupted. 'You'd have done the same...'

And he lay back.

CHAPTER 9

A DESPERATE JOURNEY

MELLOR WAS very skilled in first aid, and he found that Bruce's injuries were less severe than expected. The bones were only badly wrenched, not actually broken; a few hours' massage worked wonders, and within two or three days the wrenched ankles showed signs of healing. Even so, Mellor firmly forbade Bruce to make any attempt to stand.

'If we try to gain a day, we may lose a month,' he said once, when Bruce had been unusually persistent. 'I know it's infuriating to have to lie back and do nothing, but we can't make any sort of a move until you feel fit for a long walk. We may have to cover a couple of hundred miles all told. Even if Maurice feels like carrying you back again, I don't!'

Maurice, for his part, felt restless. He recovered quickly from the effects of his ordeal, since in spite of his slim figure he was as tough as whipcord, but he longed to be doing something definite instead of just waiting. In general he slept during the Martian daytime, when Mellor - in spite of his earlier pronouncement to the contrary - was making desperate and unsuccessful attempts to patch up the wrecked navigation computer boards, and spent the hours of darkness sitting at the communications console tapping out periodical messages in the vain hope of receiving some reply from Leslie Yorke. Now and then he took advantage of the hours of daylight to go outside on to the plain.

The two moons were fascinating to see. One of them, Phobos, seemed to scurry along, moving almost perceptibly; the other, Deimos, stayed almost still. Neither was brilliant; Deimos looked like little more than a large, fairly bright star.

On one occasion Mellor came out, and gazed up. 'Funny pair, aren't they? Not a bit like our Moon.'

'What distance are they?'

'Only a few thousand miles. Deimos - that's the fainter one - goes round Mars in about the same time as Mars spins, so it stays above the horizon for two and a half days at a time, but it's less than ten miles across. Once we've set up base here, I expect we'll use it as a sort of natural space-station.'

It was three days more before Mellor would allow Bruce to stand up and before his ankles had strengthened enough for him to go for a short hobble outside the *Ares*. Gradually his muscles recovered, and he was able to walk in comfort without holding on to Maurice or Mellor; within a week he was almost back to normal, little the worse for his fall. 'It must be something in the Martian air,' he said once. 'I remember spraining my wrist when I was a kid, and I felt it for months afterwards!' Meantime, there was nothing to be done except wait. Mellor gave up all attempts to repair the navigation equipment, and the radio remained obstinately silent. Not only was it impossible to call up the *Hermes*, but they were hopelessly out of touch even with the Earth.

'Two nights more,' said Mellor finally. 'If nothing happens by then, we shall have to chance it. You take the first watch, Maurice, and I'll relieve you about midnight.'

Maurice had become thoroughly used to the monotonous, dreary hissing of the radio, but when he switched on, just about the time when the sun was sinking below the horizon, he found that there was a difference. Instead of being loud and regular, the hissing was softer and uncertain. Now and then it would rise almost to a scream, and then it would die away altogether. Mellor joined him at the console, and grunted thoughtfully. 'I wonder,' he said. 'It may be nothing of importance, but - well, it's just possible that the Layer is clearing away again, which may give us a few hours to get hold of either Woomera or Yorke. Keep alert, and send out a call every three or four minutes.'

Maurice settled down to his watch, and waited. For some hours nothing happened; Bruce and Mellor lay down on their couches and slept, and the cabin of the *Ares* was almost as silent as the dark dust-desert outside. And then, suddenly, Maurice heard something new. Hardly daring to breathe, he gasped out a warning that brought his companions awake and to their feet, and sent out a quick, clear Morse signal:

'*Ares* calling. Repeat message, repeat message.'

A pause. Somewhere in the background Maurice could hear what sounded like Morse, but not distinctly enough for him to read it; frantically he had the computer search for a stronger signal, and called again. This time the reply was louder, and there could be no mistake:

'Yorke calling *Ares*. Can hear you. Oxygen almost exhausted. Position...'

All three listeners strained their ears, but at the critical moment the message faded, and the background flared up again. Mellor cursed under his breath, and bit his lips savagely, while Maurice re-calibrated again with steady hands and called up:

'Repeat position. Repeat position. Over.'

Again came the distant signals, but once more they were too distorted to read, and Maurice looked up quickly.

'Want to take over, David?' he muttered.

Mellor shook his head. 'You're better at this than I am. Try again, for Heaven's sake!'

Maurice clenched his teeth, and sent: 'Repeat position. Repeat position. Over.'

Another pause, during which the Morse from the *Hermes* seemed to be lost altogether. Then it was back again, fainter than before; the persistent hissing had increased, and was becoming more regular.

'Don't send again,' muttered Mellor. 'Wait.'

Hiss... crackle... Normally Maurice would have turned the volume down; but now he kept it at maximum, straining his ears as he had never strained them before. For perhaps ten seconds the hissing subsided, and he could make out the fragment of a message:

'Two days. Then...'

The Morse was lost in a violent crackle that made all three men wince as though they had been struck, and the hiss returned with its normal steady, monotonous persistence. For another two hours they remained listening, ready every moment for something new, but there was nothing, and it was only too obvious what had happened. The Violet Layer had re-formed with its usual suddenness, and they might have to wait for weeks before they had another chance of making radio contact. At last Mellor took off his headpiece, and motioned to the others to do the same.

They studied the computer recordings of the

transmissions. After half an hour, Mellor said wearily, 'Well, there we are or, rather, there we aren't. Of all the bad luck! Another ten seconds, and Yorke would have let us know whether the original position he gave us was right or not. As things are, after listening again and after computer analysis of all the Morse we received, even of what we might not have heard at the time, we still don't have their updated position. We may have to spend days searching for them.'

'What did he mean by 'two days'?' muttered Maurice, though in his heart he knew. 'The oxygen?'

'I don't imagine there's much doubt about it. Well, at least we know what we're up against,' said Mellor grimly. 'They're still alive, or at least Yorke is, and we have just about forty-eight hours in which to find them. We've lost valuable time, but if we keep up a steady four miles an hour, which will be as much as we can manage, we'll reach their estimated position in... in just about twenty-five hours, which gives us another twenty-five to locate the *Hermes*. If we fail, they'll die.'

Bruce drummed his hand against the table. 'Do you reckon they'll come out searching for us, now they know we're here? If they do, we're almost certain to miss them.'

'If they've any sense, they'll stay where they are,' said Mellor. 'When you're resting, you can manage on far less oxygen than if you're taking even gentle

exercise, and their obvious course of action is to lie
back and wait for us to get to them. The trouble is that
we'll have to take extra oxygen with us. We'll fill every
back pack we have, and trust to luck that we can keep
going. If only we knew just where they are! There's no
way of signalling...' He paused, suddenly. 'Or is
there...?'

'What do you mean?'

'I must be mad,' breathed Mellor. 'Radio's useless -
but the Violet Layer can't block light. That just might
be an answer. It's a long shot, but it may be worth a
try.'

Bruce stared. 'Light? How can that work?'

'The laser. Before now we've sent laser beams all
the way from Earth to Mars, for measuring distances
very accurately. Yorke carries a laser - and so do we.'

Maurice looked at Mellor in amazement. 'But - if
they're miles off, how can we see their laser?'

Mellor pointed upward. 'Out there. Deimos - it's
well within laser range. We just might try to use it as a
reflector. Outside.'

Bruce and Maurice climbed into their space-suits,
and made their way through the air-locks; Mellor
followed, carrying what seemed to be a case no larger
than a portable laptop computer. Next he carried out a
tripod, and set the laser up. 'Thank Heaven our
electrics still work. Watch out.'

It was an eerie scene. The night was pitch-dark;

Phobos had set, and only the stars blazed out, with Deimos glowing like a tiny disk. Maurice watched.

'How far out is it?' he muttered to Bruce. 'Hundreds of miles?'

'Nearer ten thousand,' said Bruce, his eyes turned skyward. 'All the same, this beam's powerful enough - and the system can self-position and aim itself after we enter co-ordinates.' There was a long silence. 'That's about it,' said Mellor softly. 'Here goes.' He pulled a switch, and Maurice saw a needle-thin beam shoot out from the projector; it was reddish, and seemed to stretch out towards Deimos. Mellor worked the little keypad so as to set the beam to go on and off intermittently.

'If only they see it - keep watching!'

Maurice turned his binoculars towards Deimos. He could make out the pale disk, and could see the red dot from their laser blinking on Deimos, on and then off. He concentrated; a few minutes went by... Could there be any hope? Suddenly he gave a yell. There were two red dots. 'David, look! They've seen it!'

There was no doubt; another red spot on Deimos was 'winking' back, and Maurice realized that the 'winks' weren't random. 'Morse...' He waited. 'This is it - 'Are in Arago C... Are in Arago C.' What... what can that mean?'

'It means that they've given us their position,' rapped Mellor. 'Arago C is a tiny crater right inside Aeria, where we know they came down. It can't be more than a hundred miles off. We've a chance after all - Maurice, signal them we're coming!'

It did not take long to collect what they needed. Food was easy; the concentrated high-energy liquids were in containers that snapped on to pouches on the outside of the space-suits, and the contents drawn in by straw-like tubes in the helmet of the space-suit. Water was carried and accessed the same way. They had enough supplies of both to last them for as long as they were likely to be away from the *Ares*, and the internal environmental controls of the space-suits were sufficient to deal with all body-waste functions for the journey. Weight restrictions had prevented the astronauts from bringing any type of rover vehicle, and so the supplies would have to be carried, especially the all-important oxygen, plus the small but powerful laser laptop transmitter. A final check of the suits, and Mellor led the way into the air-locks.

Bruce and Maurice followed staring silently as the pressure gauge swung over to zero. The second air-lock too was emptied, and then Mellor swung open the outer door, stepping into the blackness of the Martian night. Maurice paused for a second to take a last look at the friendly walls of the *Ares*, and then he gripped Bruce's shoulder and stepped through the door. He knew only too well that he might be saying a final 'good-bye' to the strange craft that had carried him across fifty million miles of space.

CHAPTER 10
ACROSS THE DESERT

THERE WAS hardly any twilight on Mars; it was still deep night, and though the sun could not be far below the horizon there was not the faintest glimmer of dawn along the skyline. Instead, the stars shone down with a steely radiance, hard and unwinking.

Deimos was there, while low down in the south could be seen a bright bluish object, brighter than any star, which Maurice knew to be his own Earth. Would he ever be able to return?

Mellor was in no mood for loitering. As soon as he had closed the hull door, so that it was secure against any dust-storm that might spring up, he set out across the desert, the torch attached to his waist-belt casting a cone of radiance on to the ochre ground. Bruce was in even more of a hurry, and was some ten yards ahead when the scientist called him back.

'Steady on,' he said, curtly. 'There's no sense in trying to rush. We've got many miles to go, and if we try to go too quickly we'll merely wear ourselves out. Much better to keep up an ordinary walking pace; it's the most we can hope for.'

'I suppose you're right,' grunted Bruce, and slackened his pace to a steady walk. 'What worries me most is how we're ever going to find our way back again, even if we do have the luck to stumble across Yorke straight away. There are no landmarks to guide us, *Ares'* homing beacon doesn't work and the compasses won't do anything except go round in circles because of the Violet Layer.

'The point hadn't escaped me,' said Mellor drily. 'In fact, I've spent most of the last fortnight racking my brains about it. I can't pretend to have hit on a full solution, because there isn't one, but I have worked out a scheme that may help. If not, we shall have to manage as well as we can by taking bearings of the sun and the stars.'

Maurice looked curious. 'What's the scheme, then?'

'Theseus and the Minotaur.' In spite of everything, Mellor chuckled. 'I can see you don't know much about the old Greek legends, so I'll explain. Theseus was a hero who had to find his way through a gigantic maze in order to reach a bull-like monster called the Minotaur. To help him find his way out again, he dragged a silken cord after him to mark the passages he'd passed through. I haven't a silken cord, I'm afraid, but I have got these.' He waved his gloved hand, and indicated the large plastic box fixed to his waist-belt. 'This box holds four hundred extremely powerful electro-magnets, about the size of small dice. The lab boys fixed them up for me at Woomera before we left. Every few hundred yards I'm going to switch one on and drop it. Their cell power is enough for about 3 days, and so they will outlast our oxygen supply; whatever happens, that should be long enough. There's our compass bearing for the way back, and there's our trail.'

Bruce looked uncertain. 'It... well, it sounds all right, but surely no ordinary compass will be able to follow a track like that?'

Mellor shrugged. 'It all depends on conditions. If there's no magnetic material in the ground itself I think it will, and in any case we shall be able to see the cubes themselves as they have a light in them; provided that there isn't another dust-storm before we come back, of course. All we really want to do is to make sure we're heading in the right direction. Sun and star bearings will keep us in a straight line all right, and the *Ares* itself is so strongly magnetized that the compass will lead us to it once we're within a radius of a couple of miles, Violet Layer or no Violet Layer. Anyhow, it's the best I can do.'

For hours they tramped on through the darkened desert, pausing every now and then for Mellor to place one of his cubes upon a heaped-up pile of ochre material; 'building dust-castles', Maurice called it. Phobos dipped below the horizon; Deimos remained, and now and then Maurice scanned it with his binoculars, but there were no more signals.

'How long to sunrise?' asked Bruce, at last.

'Not more than twenty minutes,' said Mellor briefly. 'The daylight will hit us suddenly when it does come. I doubt whether the dawn will last for more than five minutes at the outside.'

In this he was correct. One minute, it was still pitch dark; the next, a shaft of light had appeared along the eastern horizon, turning the blackness into mauve, and slowly the shrunken white disk of the sun came into view, while all the stars faded away like chalk-marks upon a slate which is being wiped clean. Once again they could see far across the ochre desert, but the view was much the same as before. Miles ahead they could make out some more of the low, rounded dust-hills, while the *Ares* had dropped far below the horizon astern.

'How're you doing?' said Mellor, pausing. 'We shall have to take a rest soon, I suppose, but I'd rather leave it until we've got to the top of those hills.'

Bruce and Maurice nodded, and once again they plodded on, each occupied with thoughts of their own. They seemed to have left all traces of the green mineral deposits behind, and ahead there was nothing but the reddish felsites and the blue-mauve vault of the sky.

The hills ahead were higher than those that Bruce and Maurice had crossed some days before, and their slopes were steeper, so that by the time they reached the crest of a pass between two of the peaks the sun had risen high in the sky. Bruce's ankles ached; Maurice felt horribly tired, and it came as a great relief when Mellor called a halt.

'Rest,' he said. 'Ten minutes before we start off again. Make the most of it.'

He sprawled flat on the ground, relaxing wearily inside his uncomfortable space-suit, and the other two followed his example, lying back and breathing hard. Maurice blew out his cheeks. 'Phew!' he said, half to himself. 'I never did care much for hiking!' He stared upward, and then he was struck with a sudden idea.

'David!'

Mellor stirred. 'Yes?'

'See that peak there? It's a bit higher than the rest. If I climb up on to the top of it, it might be some help with the radio. I mean, we would have a better chance of getting in touch with the *Hermes* again.'

'I doubt it, but at this stage of the game anything's worth trying,' said Mellor, and sat up. 'I ought to have thought of it myself. I don't expect the radio will be of any use if the Violet Layer is as noisy as usual, but we might be lucky. Shall I go, or do you feel up to it?'

'It was my idea,' said Maurice, and hauled himself to his feet. 'It won't take me more than ten minutes to get to the top, and I'll be in full view all the way.'

Leaving Bruce and Mellor spread out on the ground, he set off towards the crest of the peak. 'Peak' was hardly the right word; 'bulge' would have been better, as there was nothing very mountainous about the rounded dust-hill. Now and then his feet seemed to sink more deeply into the ground, but nothing unusual occurred, and presently he had reached the highest point of the entire range of hills. As before, he could see nothing of interest. To the north and south, the hills lowered into the plain; to the east and west there was nothing but the monotonous redness, and he switched his transmitter to full power, hoping against hope for an answer.

'*Ares* calling Dr. Yorke. *Ares* calling Dr. Yorke. Over!'

Hiss... crackle... The Layer was in good voice, thought Maurice ruefully, and he called again, this time operating the Morse key of his suit with his practised hand. Still there was no response, and Mellor's voice sounded in his headphones.

'It's no use, Maurice. Better come back; it's time to get moving.'

Regretfully Maurice switched off and started to walk back down the slope. He had covered perhaps half the distance - when the ground seemed to fall away beneath his feet, and he let out a shout. Next moment he felt a powerful sucking pressure drawing him downwards, and realized with sick horror that he was being drawn down into the dust...

'Bruce! David!' he shouted wildly, scrabbling at the grip-less dust with his hands. 'Look out! It's a... a quicksand!'

'Hold on!' roared Bruce, and dimly Maurice saw that his two companions were racing towards him. Still came that relentless sucking; now Maurice was buried up to his knees, and struggle as he might he could do nothing to free himself from the vice-like grip. Bruce and Mellor seemed to be coming onwards in slow motion, bounding high in the air and falling with ominous gentleness under the slight pressure of Martian gravity... He was almost waist-deep, and fought desperately to keep calm.

'Careful!' he shouted, his voice rising almost to a scream. 'It may get you, too... It's all round me!'

Bruce, in the lead, was close now - only a few yards to go, and then Maurice realized that the dust ahead was equally treacherous. Bruce staggered, and his metal boots sank into the redness.

Maurice choked. 'You can't get me. Keep away!'

Bruce did not reply. Desperately he flung himself forwards, falling flat on his face and reaching out until his hand hooked into Maurice's belt just above the level of the quicksand. Behind him, Mellor judged the edge of the firm ground to the nearest foot, and gripped hold of Bruce's legs... For minutes on end they hung there, the combined pull of the two men just balancing the suction that was trying to pull Maurice to his death.

Maurice gave a sobbing gasp. 'You can't do it! Bruce, you'll never do it!'

Bruce gritted his teeth, and wrenched with every ounce of his strength. Mellor panted and gasped; was it imagination, or was Maurice starting to move? A few seconds more, and he felt a heartfelt surge of relief; slowly but surely the boy was being pulled out of the deadly quicksand, and abruptly the suction relaxed. Maurice plunged headlong forward, and he and Bruce rolled to the safety of the hard, dust-covered ground. It was some time before any of them could speak.

At last Bruce sat up, and gasped. 'What... what the devil was it?'

'It was trying to suck me down,' muttered Maurice. Sweat was running down his face; never before had he known such ghastly fear, even when lost in outer space or caught by the dust-storm. 'It felt almost as though it were alive!'

Mellor glanced quickly at the brownish, innocent looking ground above them. 'Get back down into the valley,' he ordered, picking himself up. 'From now on, we'll have to keep clear of the hills. I don't believe they're real mountains at all; they're just tremendous dust-drifts, heaped by the winds. The plain itself seems to be firm enough, thank Heaven. All right, Maurice?'

Maurice swallowed hard, and nodded. He knew that

he would never forget those hideous minutes in the quicksand, and even when they had left the hills far behind, so that they appeared as nothing more than slight swellings near the horizon, he kept on casting his eyes back towards them. Mars was full of surprises, he reflected grimly; storms, the Violet Layer, and now this deadly, sucking horror. He set his jaw, and plodded steadily on.

It was mid-day now, with the sun high in the heavens, and all three began to feel a little tired and also a little warm. Mellor estimated the temperature as being well over 40 degrees Fahrenheit, and while their suits were insulated, each with its own internal environmental control, they could - and did - absorb the solar radiation, and in addition each individual was exerting a sustained and continuous effort. Maurice's inner clothes were lathered with sweat, and his head ached furiously. Bruce was having severe trouble with his ankles, but in spite of the pain he said nothing. Now, of all times, he had to keep going. As the hours passed, and the sun sank down towards the horizon, the afternoon chill descended again, and once more Phobos could be seen, shining down from the purple background like a miniature crescent moon.

'How far do you reckon we've come?' asked Maurice at last, as Mellor paused in order to build another 'dust-castle' to hold one of his electro-magnetic cubes. 'Seems to me we can't be a long way from where Uncle Leslie said he was.'

Mellor grunted. 'Don't you believe it. We've been walking for just about twelve hours, and we cover something like four miles an hour. That makes a total of less than fifty miles, and it's a hundred to the *Hermes*. Frankly, I'm not sure that all the high-energy liquids in the world can make us do it unless we stop and have a certain amount of sleep. We may lose time in trying to carry on non-stop.'

Bruce gave a groan. 'I... I don't believe I can do another fifty miles, David. You two keep going, if you like.'

Mellor paused, and then made up his mind. 'It's easier to move by day than by night, even if it is rather too warm for comfort. We'll do our best to carry on walking until about ten o'clock, which will take us another twenty to twenty-five miles, and then we'll just have to risk it and go to sleep. We shall have to cut it as short as possible, but even two or three hours will make all the difference.'

Maurice began to feel strangely light-headed. As he walked on, his eyes fixed on Mellor's figure a few yards ahead, he began to imagine that he could see things in the desert: oases, and palm-trees, and castles; yet he knew that in reality there was nothing but the ochre dust, and he shook himself angrily. They crossed another range of hills, taking good care to keep to the passes between the peaks, and over miles more of the reddish wilderness. Just about the time of sunset, they began to meet with isolated patches of the greenish mineral, while in the distance they could just make out a more extensive area of greenness.

Mellor pointed. 'See that? It's the beginning of the dark area of the Deltaton Sinus. Frankly I'm glad to see it, because it shows me that we're just about where I thought we were. We go northwards now, and if Yorke's position was correct the *Hermes* should be in the Arago C crater, around twenty miles away.'

The greenish mineral seemed to be more concentrated and greener than that which Bruce and Maurice had seen in their earlier venture, but there was no time to reach it before the sun set; almost at once, the landscape became darker than the darkest Earth night. Phobos and Deimos between them could do no more than cast a pale, ghostly radiance like that of a crescent moon, and once again all three had to rely upon their powerful torches. The hours dragged, and Maurice, for one, began to wonder whether his strength would be equal to the last part of the journey. Every muscle felt utterly weary, and he was about to say something when Mellor stopped. 'Ten o'clock,' he said. 'If we don't have some rest, we'll never make it. The trouble is that we daren't all go to sleep at the same time, or we might waste twelve hours instead of three. We'll have to take it in turns - two asleep, and one on guard.'

'I'll take first spell,' said Bruce quietly. 'How long?'

'An hour; we can't afford more. Then you wake me, and I'll give it another hour before calling Maurice. I hate staying still when every moment is of value, but there's no choice. If we don't, we shall just collapse.'

He lay back on the ground, and Maurice followed suit. The relief of letting his tired muscles relax was tremendous, and he breathed deeply. Inside five minutes he was sound asleep, so soundly in fact that he was beyond dreaming. The next thing he remembered was being roughly shaken, and he blinked his eyes open to find Mellor's space-suited figure standing over him.

'Time to wake up,' said Mellor. 'I've given you an extra half hour as it is, so that you'll have to wake Bruce and me in another thirty minutes. The longer we stay here, the more worried I get. For goodness sake, don't let yourself drop off again; keep walking about.'

Maurice staggered to his feet, and went to rub his eyes, forgetting for the moment that he was wearing a space-suit. It was still pitch-dark, with Phobos gone and only Deimos casting a few pale rays across the bleak landscape, but he could still see the shining, star-like Earth, and he was somehow glad of it. Before he was properly awake Mellor had stretched himself out again, and all was silent.

More from habit than from hope, Maurice tuned his radio and sent out a call to the *Hermes*, but the persistent hissing of the Violet Layer drowned any possible reply, and after perhaps ten minutes he gave it

up. The sleep, short though it had been, had done him
good, and even though he still felt weary he knew that
he could face another long walk.

CHAPTER 11

A MESSAGE FROM DEIMOS

BY THE time that Mellor, Bruce and Maurice were ready to start, the stars had begun to fade from the sky. Dawn came quickly to Mars. The Earth could no longer be seen, and Deimos was barely visible as a pale disk against the pinkness. There was almost no wind, but by now even Mellor was starting to feel the strain of staying inside his space-suit. 'Wish I could have a bath,' commented Maurice. 'I've never felt so grubby in my life!'

Onward they went, leaving the 'Theseus Cord' behind them. Once Bruce stumbled, and for a moment Maurice cast his mind back to the dust-storm; he had no wish to go through that again - carrying Bruce would have been out of the question. When they paused to rest, after another hour or so, a thought struck Maurice.

'Will the laser beam work during the daytime?'

'The laser will work,' said Mellor, 'but I don't think it could light up Deimos brightly enough for us to see it

- and the same goes for *Hermes*. No, we'll have to navigate as well as we can. The one saving grace is that I know exactly were Arago C is on the maps, and it isn't large, so that if the *Hermes* is inside it we ought to find it easily enough.'

'Once we've found the crater,' said Bruce.

'Quite so. That's our main problem. In a way it's a pity that Mars has practically no proper magnetic field, but if we can cope with that damned Violet Layer we should be all right; the compass needle will lead us straight to the *Hermes*. I don't suppose there are any other metal space-ships around here!'

Four hours... five... six. Maurice was horribly tired, but he knew that he had to keep on. Again they rested, and Mellor lay back wearily. 'Well, according to my calculations we ought to reach Arago C in another seven hours - provided that I've got my sums right. That means we will have to do the last lap in the dark. By then it'll be time to start taking notice of our surroundings instead of just staring at our feet. Maurice, keep the radio on all the time. The crackle will probably deafen you, but that can't be helped. Keep calling.'

It was an hour later that Maurice saw something unusual, and he stopped. 'Look at this, what do you reckon it is?'

A few yards to his left there was what looked uncannily like a bone. Mellor went over and stirred it with his foot. Then he gave a gasp of amazement. Not only was there a bone, but also there were others.

'A skeleton,' said Bruce. 'A fossil - a genuine Martian at last. Boy! What will they make of this back home!'

'If we get home,' said Mellor grimly, 'and just at the moment I wouldn't bank on that. But do you realize what this means? There *has* been life on Mars - and not only creepy-crawlies; this looks to me like an animal of some kind, and I don't believe it's millions of years old. If it went back that far, it would have been buried in the dust.'

'Can there be any life now, then?'

'Who knows? Oh, well,' said Mellor. 'No point in speculating now. We'll have plenty of time later if we manage to locate the *Hermes*. On our way.'

If Maurice had been tired before, he was doubly so now, and as the sky began to darken he couldn't help wondering how much longer he could last. He knew that both Bruce and Mellor felt the same, but time was running out. At this moment Yorke, Whitton and Knight might be using up the last of their precious oxygen...

The hills sank into the horizon behind them, and again they made their way across a seemingly unending plain, broken only by low, gentle swells here and there. As time passed, Bruce and Mellor paused more often to search the skyline with their binoculars, always hoping to see some sign of the metal hull of the *Hermes*, but without success, and at last Maurice realized that the hands of his watch had moved on to eleven o'clock. They had arrived almost at the bottom of yet another line of hills, rounded and low like all the rest.

Mellor stopped, took bearings of the Sun and Phobos, and then referred to his map. 'Yes,' he said, softly. 'Just as I thought. This is where they said they'd come down. I may be five or six miles out, but not more. Well, what do we do?'

'If you know for certain they're pretty close to us...' began Maurice.

'That's the trouble; I don't. All I know is that this is where they said they were. Remember, Yorke sent that message pretty soon after he landed, and with a wrecked ship and a suspect communications system I doubt whether he'd had time to make a proper check, especially if they realized the Violet Layer had suddenly cleared for a while and they wanted to get a message out quickly. If he's really inside Arago C it will be all right but I don't suppose he's really sure, and we've only about twenty-five hours left. After that it'll be too late.'

Bruce bit his lip. 'Does it mean splitting up, then? Can't say I fancy that!'

'It doesn't mean anything of the sort, as you'd realize if you took the trouble to think. When I originally said we'd have to separate, I didn't bargain for this sort of position. We know for a fact that Yorke, Whitton and Knight are desperately short of oxygen, which means that they'll have to take some of ours. If any one of us went hunting on our own, and did happen to stumble across the *Hermes*, there still wouldn't be enough oxygen to go round. We shall have to pool all we've got, and even then it'll be a near thing. If only we could use the radio!'

'Well, we can't,' said Bruce shortly, 'and that's that. Sure we can't use the laser yet?'

'Not a chance. We'll have to wait till dark, and even then it will be difficult enough'. Mellor gave a sudden grin. 'You know, I've been working out the odds against Yorke having seen our signal. He, or one of the others, must have been looking at Deimos at that very moment, and at a guess I'd say that the odds were less than one in ten thousand - even if he tumbled to the fact that we might try the beam.'

'They'll be watching now, though?'

'Yes, I would think so. I only wish I had a more accurate fix on our position. I doubt if I'm more than thirty miles out, but even that might be too much. We've got to hope that we find Arago C first time, and that the *Hermes* really is inside it. Luckily the crater's only four miles across.'

'Sure of that?'

'Yes. Remember the Mars Odyssey probe - the space-ship that went round and round Mars in 2003?

That sent back very close-range pictures, and Arago C is unmistakable. It's one of the impact craters, formed when a chunk of rock ploughed into Mars millions of years ago.'

Sunset - and still there was no sign of anything but the featureless desert; all the high volcanoes of Mars were many miles away. Not that they were active now; they had last roared in the distant past, but they showed that Mars had once been an active as well as a possible life-bearing world. The radio was useless; the Violet Layer was in full cry. Twice they stopped to keep a watch on Deimos, but with no result.

'How long, David?' asked Maurice at last.

'Not long enough. Keep watching, all of you.'

It was Bruce who saw the first flash, and he gave a shout. 'That's it - they're sending!'

Deimos was indeed flashing, and much more violently than before; it was almost as though a light was being shone from the satellite itself. Maurice said out loud for them all, "Arago C, Arago C. Hurry, hurry'.'

Then the flashes stopped, and Deimos glowed steadily.

'Clever,' breathed Mellor. 'See? It was the eastern side that is being lit up - so that's the direction we'll have to take. If that's right, we ought to see the crater walls in three or four hours. If we don't - well it'll be the end for them.'

The next part of the journey was even more nerve-wracking. Both Bruce and Maurice were feeling the strain more than they would have cared to admit, and even Mellor was beginning to flag. Maurice lost all count of time; it was only when the sky began to lighten, and the dark mauve was replaced by pink, that he realized that Mellor's 'three or four hours' were past.

'Keep going,' said Mellor hoarsely. 'I may be mad, but I believe there's something ahead.' He pointed. 'It could be the crater wall.'

They reached the foot of a long slope, and began to climb. The gradient was not steep, but even so it made the going more difficult, and Maurice had to realize that he could do little more. But then, suddenly, Mellor called, 'Dead ahead. It's a light! Hurry!'

Bruce and Maurice needed no urging. For the next ten minutes all three forgot the need to save every scrap of oxygen; all their attention was concentrated on the flickering, gleaming point that seemed to lie so far ahead. Maurice's heart pounded as he ran. This must be their last chance - could it be nothing more than a mirage in the desert?

After a few moments more there could be no doubt. Standing up from the ground, its hull glinting a pale grey, and slanting at a crazy angle, lay a flattened, double pear-shaped body that might have been a second *Ares*, and a light flashed as the beam of a torch swung towards them.

Gasping and panting, Mellor plunged up towards the stranded spacecraft, and reached out towards the space-suited figure that stood before the air-lock staring at him as though he had been a ghost. Even above the background hiss, they could hear a wild exclamation. 'Mellor! Great Heaven! Whitton - Knight! Be quick!'

'Leslie! How many of you are alive?' said Mellor.

'All of us - just,' said Leslie Yorke, in a dry, cracked voice. 'David, I just can't believe it. I'm crazy - I must be crazy. It's impossible!'

Maurice pounded up as the air-lock swung open and two more men dropped on to the desert. 'Uncle Leslie! It's me - Maurice,' he said breathlessly. 'Are you all right?'

'Maurice? Maurice who?' Yorke stared stupidly. 'I don't know any Maurice's except... Heavens above, this is becoming madder and madder every moment!'

CHAPTER 12
THE
THESEUS
CORD

INSIDE THE *Hermes*, after the great greetings and exchange of stories, and a little rest, Mellor brought up the vital situation of the *Ares*.

'Listen carefully, Leslie,' he said grimly. 'When we landed in the *Ares*, just over a fortnight ago, we smashed our navigation equipment. It was something to do with that infernal Violet Layer, I think. Otherwise, the ship's space-worthy.' He paused. 'It all depends on this. Is your own navigation system serviceable? If so, we can take it back with us, and fit it to the *Ares*. Otherwise, we're all here for good.'

An American voice broke in. Norman Knight thrust himself forward. 'I guess our navigation mother boards and computers were about the only things we didn't smash. The main controls are matchwood, and so are the drive circuits, but the navigation's OK - as far as I know.'

Mellor drew a deep breath. 'Then we've still a

chance.'

'What's the oxygen position, David?' asked Yorke.

'We've enough to last the three of you and us for about sixty hours,' said Mellor, 'which ought to be enough to get us all back to the *Ares*.'

'We've supplies for about ten hours more inside the *Hermes*,' added Professor Whitton quietly, laying his hand on Mellor's shoulder. 'About half an hour before you appeared, we were sinuously discussing whether it would be best to walk outside, open our helmets and get it over with quickly; we didn't believe that we had a chance in a million. We'll never be able to repay you.'

Mellor grunted. 'We're not home yet by a long way, Charles. Don't forget that taking off with six aboard is going to be a tricky business, even though two of us are lightweights.' He turned to Knight. 'How long will it take you to dismantle your navigation systems?'

'An hour - no more,' drawled the American, his eyes looking round the *Hermes*. 'Boy, will I be glad to say good-bye to this bucket of bolts! I reckoned we were here for keeps, and no mistake.'

'We very nearly were,' said Leslie Yorke. 'So this is the nephew I've heard about, but never met...' He had a humourous-looking face partly hidden by a pointed black beard. 'What in the name of reason made you come on a journey like this?'

'I had to,' said Maurice simply. 'I was the only communications operator who didn't weigh too much.

I guess I'm a bit lighter still now - I must have sweated off pounds during the last day or two!'

Yorke shook his head in bewilderment, but said no more; clearly, he was still dazed by the sudden turn of events. Charles Whitton, younger and quiet-mannered, took everything in his stride, and Norman Knight was much too busy for the next couple of hours to say much to anybody. With Bruce to help him, he systematically removed all the navigation mother boards, computer chips, circuits and connections from their positions in the *Hermes*, and stacked them in readiness for departure, placing the vital systems with great care in two metal cases. Yorke, Whitton and Mellor talked as they worked, comparing notes and arguing as calmly as though they had been seated comfortably inside the lounge at Woomera Headquarters; Maurice lay back upon a couch and closed his eyes. He had been on the alert now for so long that he was almost beyond the stage of tiredness, but he knew that the greatest effort of all still lay ahead.

Eventually he fell asleep, and woke some time later at the touch of Bruce's hand. The cabin of the *Hermes* looked different. Some of the complicated equipment had been ripped out, and so had the oxygen tubes, while the main oxygen container hung loosely open. Maurice stared at it. He knew something about the system of renewing and circulating the precious gas, but in the *Ares* the largest containers had been sealed off.

'Is it empty?' he asked, rubbing his eyes.

Professor Whitton nodded. 'It is indeed. As I told you, we had enough for about ten hours more. Well, we've drawn all that off into smaller packs, so that in a few minutes the air inside here will become unfit to breathe without masks. We're about ready.'

Maurice yawned. 'Phew! I'd just dropped off... How are things going?'

'All right so far,' said Leslie Yorke, dropping a hand on Maurice's shoulder. 'You know, I still can't get over you of all people turning up in this extraordinary way. I've a feeling that you're the kind of nephew I want. Still,' he added, 'we'll have plenty of time to find out something about each other on the way back. Better get into your suit.'

Maurice obeyed. Whitton, Knight and Mellor were already encased inside their stiff space-suits; Bruce and Maurice followed - already the air in the cabin was becoming difficult to breathe and for the last time, the crew of the *Hermes* looked round at the cabin that had been their home for more than a year.

'I'm sorry we have to leave it here,' said Yorke, in an undertone. 'It's done all we could ask of it.'

Knight snorted. 'Maybe, except getting us home again, and that's what counts! Let's get moving, Les. Our oxygen won't last for ever.'

Yorke nodded without replying. Silently they passed straight through the air-locks - there was no point now in waiting for the pumps to exhaust the atmosphere inside - and stepped out on to the dark plain. Maurice looked around, but there was no sign of a living thing, and to all appearances Mars was a dead world.

Bruce paused. 'Which way, David? Do you reckon we can work our way back by the stars?'

'I hope so,' said Mellor grimly. 'I had no time to do more than switch on and drop my electro-magnetic cubes as we came along in the end, but I didn't waste my time. About twenty miles east of us we'll find a mountain range, with a couple of squarish peaks that look rather like sugar loaves. After that we turn almost due south, and with any luck we'll either come to a region we recognize, or stumble across some of our dust-castles. Don't talk more than you must, and breathe as deeply as you can.'

If anything, Maurice thought that the journey back was even more nerve-racking than the outward trip. True, they no longer had the gnawing anxiety of wondering whether they would reach the *Hermes* to find nothing but a huddled group of lifeless bodies, but they had more to carry; Yorke and Whitton had shouldered the navigation equipment between them, which left the others to deal with all the oxygen packs and other necessities - and they were feeling weary and sore. After all, they had walked a hundred miles almost non-stop, and even under the lessened gravity such a trek was no mean feat.

By sunrise, they had reached the mountain range that Mellor had spoken about. They turned southwards, and for what seemed eternity they marched on, away from the green mineral scrub and back into the heart of the ochre desert. Twice they had to pause for short rests, and Mellor noted with some anxiety that neither Yorke nor Whitton was in good shape. Yorke in particular was panting painfully, and he staggered as he walked.

'Feel bad, Les?' said Knight softly.

Yorke nodded. 'I... I do, I'm afraid. I'm not sure that I shall be able to carry on much longer. If not, you'll have to leave me to make as good a time as I can.'

'After coming fifty million miles to fetch you, we're not likely to leave you now,' said Bruce drily. 'Give me that metal box with the navigation system, Leslie. I can manage a bit more.'

'So can I,' put in Maurice, though inwardly he did not feel so sure. 'I'm fit for anything.'

Yorke protested, but Bruce and Maurice firmly removed the case from him and divided the carrying of it between them. Knight later had less to carry, as from time to time as they progressed empty oxygen back-packs were changed for the full ones Knight was carrying, and so he took over the carrying of the other radar case from Whitton for a while. Meanwhile, Mellor was checking their position as well as he could. The compass was useless so far; either they were some way from the 'Theseus Cord', or else the powerful attraction of the Violet Layer was drawing the needle so much that his desperate scheme was doomed to failure.

By mid-day they had crossed two more ranges of hills, but still no familiar landmarks came in sight. 'Don't forget that we covered a good many miles in the dark, though,' Mellor reminded them on one of the rare occasions when he spoke. 'At least we're heading in the right direction.' As they went on, Maurice's spirits fell. They had come so far, and they had accomplished so much, that it would be doubly hard to fail now.

'How much longer will the oxygen last?' said Whitton, at about sunset.

'Twelve hours,' said Mellor briefly. 'No more.'

Yorke breathed hard. 'If one or two of us stayed here, it would give the rest of you more chance,' he said. 'I feel...'

'It's all or none,' rapped Mellor. 'We're not in any trouble yet, and we can cover another forty miles or so before the position starts to get really serious. Keep going, all of you, and don't talk.'

To Maurice, the going down of the sun had a new significance. By the time it rose again, they would either have found the *Ares*, or... He did not like to think what might have happened. As he watched the whitish disk sink from view, he could not help wondering whether he would be alive to see it rise again. Bruce's hand touched him gently on the arm, and Maurice forced a grin. 'We've done our best, pal,' he heard Bruce say quietly. 'I reckon it's been worth while.' Still they struggled on, while the darkness gathered and the blue Earth shone down, looking tantalizingly near.

Yorke gasped painfully. 'I... I simply can't keep going much longer. If I collapse, you're not to wait for me.'

'If you collapse, two of us have got to carry you, and that'll make things doubly difficult,' said Mellor curtly. 'Do your best, for all our sakes.'

Midnight... one o'clock, and again Phobos rose, doing something to relieve the blackness. But time was running short now, and all of them knew it.

Suddenly, Mellor let out an exclamation.

'Look at this. I... I believe the needle's kicking!'

Bruce and Maurice leaped forward. Sure enough, the compass indicator no longer quivered and swung uncertainly; it had turned to a constant direction, and remained there even though Mellor shook the instrument violently. Maurice's heart bounded. Could the 'Theseus Cord' be near at hand after all?

It was. All six said a heartfelt prayer of thanks as after only a few more minutes, Mellor's foot almost stumbled over one of the 'dust-castles' that they had built on their outward journey. As they passed the dust-castle, Mellor picked up the cube and carefully switched it off, placing it back into the large plastic box attached to his belt. The compass needle swung away and over to the direction of the next dust-castle. The needle was steady and sure; the 'Theseus Cord' worked.

Even Yorke forgot his physical distress as they hurried along as rapidly as they could. Providentially, Phobos was almost full, giving a light equal to that of a strong crescent moon.

At last Mellor's keen eyes caught sight of a metal glint in the distance that could only be the friendly, grey-coated hull of a space-ship.

Thirty minutes later, all six were safe inside the *Ares*.

CHAPTER 13

INTO THE VIOLET LAYER

BRUCE AND Maurice stood outside the air-lock of the *Ares* and stared across the desert at the distant hills. It was a fortnight now since the end of their nightmare journey, and for them it had been a fortnight of rest, though Mellor and Norman Knight had been working at full pressure to install the equipment they had brought from the *Hermes*. It had remained impossible to call up the Earth. Indeed, they had almost stopped trying, and there was no other way in which Maurice at least could be of help.

He had slept for twenty-four hours on end after their return, and it was not until then that he realized how near he had been to breaking-point. Even Bruce, a few years older and as tough as iron, had been 'all in', as he admitted later, and Yorke had been so ill that for some time Whitton and Mellor were distinctly anxious about him. Happily the fever had passed, and within a week he too was hard at work, checking the nuclear-ion motors of the *Ares* as carefully as he could to make sure that all was ready for their launch.

Whitton had his own interests. As Maurice had learned, he was a naturalist, and he spent long hours prowling outside on the plain armed with a camera, and from time to time he came back with a bag of the strange, green mineral that was on the far side of the hills. 'I'd very much like to bring back one of the fossils,' he said regretfully, 'and I suppose even these bags of stuff will have to stay for now. Next time I come here, I'm not going home again without both, come what may.'

Maurice had looked surprised. 'Why not go and bring one in now, sir? I don't suppose anything will have run off with them.'

'Partly because I've had all the walking I want for one expedition, and partly because I couldn't bring it in any case,' said Whitton.

'You don't fully understand the position,' said Mellor seriously. 'Even though both you and Bruce are lightweights, the *Ares* is going to be dangerously overloaded when we blast away. Normally I'd say there was a fair margin of safety, but we've got to reckon with the Violet Layer. It's true that we shall be going through under full power, instead of drifting as we were last time, but even so it's impossible to tell just what the effect will be, and we can only make one attempt. If we fail, and we have to land again - well, here we stay.'

Certainly neither Mellor nor Yorke appeared particularly confident, even though they said little; and as the days went by, the tension grew. Knight finished installing and testing the navigation systems, while Bruce and Maurice spent most of their waking hours either at the communications console or outside the *Ares* until every detail of the desert scene became printed on their memories. Now that the final test was so near at hand, Maurice had to confess that he was horribly 'on edge'.

'What do you suppose the chances are?' he said, kicking idly against the reddish ground and disturbing a puff of dust that settled slowly. 'Can you get anything out of David and Uncle Leslie?'

Bruce shrugged. 'I'm no expert in nuclear-ion, but I think they reckon that the odds are about fifty-fifty. It all depends upon this infernal Violet Layer. Brace up, pal - we've been through worse times than this.'

'I'll say we have,' said Maurice, and grinned. 'I could bear anything but that ghastly quicksand. Ugh! I'll never forget that, as long as I live. Thanks for yanking me out of it.'

'I might as well thank you for dragging me back over the hills, soon after we landed,' said Bruce soberly. 'We certainly picked right when we chose you for this mission.'

Mellor's voice sounded in their headphones. 'Hello, Bruce! Hello, Bruce. Where the devil are you?'

Bruce replied. 'Just outside. Want me?'

'I want you both. We've been listening on the radio, and as you can probably tell yourselves there's been another clearing of the Layer. We can't afford to miss it - it may be our one chance to break through without meeting with any trouble. We lift off in twenty minutes from now! Hurry.'

Bruce and Maurice dived towards the air-lock. Both had heard that the background hiss had virtually disappeared, but neither had registered its significance. As the door swung open, Maurice took a last look at the ochre desert, the blue-mauve sky, the whitish sun and the distant hills; then he clambered in, scarcely waiting for the indicator to swing to 'normal' before starting to struggle out of his space-suit.

Inside the cabin, Yorke and Whitton were already strapped down on to couches, while Mellor feverishly studied the controls and Knight carried out a final inspection of the navigation computers. As Bruce and Maurice plunged in, fastening the air-lock door behind them, Mellor wheeled round.

'Get ready,' he rapped. 'We're two couches short, so you'll have to share one while Norman jams himself flat on the spare. I'd meant to fit the extra couches today, but this is a chance we dare not lose - it may not happen again for months. Listen on the radio, Maurice, for the level of static and keep reporting. Never mind about the readings; Charles will do them this time.'

Breathlessly Maurice pulled on his headset, and laid down on his side on the couch. Bruce sprawled aside him, back to back. Fortunately the straps were long enough to fasten them both, pressing Bruce's back close up against Maurice's, while Norman Knight pulled the spare couch-seat into the cabin and wedged it as tightly as he could. Mellor's hands hovered over the computer controls, and he turned.

'Five minutes. Radio, Maurice?'

'Practically nothing,' said Maurice quietly. 'The hissing isn't there. I believe you're right - the Layer has cleared!'

'Thank Heaven for that. Stand by.'

Maurice held his breath. Still there was no sound from the radio, apart from an occasional crackle; if only the clearing lasted for another five minutes, they had a real chance, and he strained his ears, half expecting the deadly hiss to return as it had done so often before. Then the computer countdown reached zero. There was a momentary pause; the motors whined and rose to a shrill scream, and as the *Ares* lurched Maurice felt again the crushing pressure of lift-off. It felt even worse this time, partly because he was already out of breath, and partly because he and Bruce were pressed up against each other, and Maurice was panting and gasping as he tried to lever himself away a little by his elbows and wrists. Dimly he heard Whitton calling out readings, and once more the red specks floated in front of his eyes. The *Ares* shuddered as though a mighty hammer had struck her, and Maurice gulped; his mouth was dry with fear, and every instant he expected the space-craft to plunge back towards Mars, smashing itself and them to atoms against the ochre desert.

'Readings!' roared Mellor, and the motors whined to a tortured crescendo, while the pressure increased still more and Maurice's body seemed to get crushed as though by a ton weight. Knight had lost his grip of the central pillar and had rolled across the cabin, kicking wildly until he collided with the opposite wall... Yorke gave a gasping cry, and Whitton's steady voice faltered.

Again the *Ares* lurched; and then, quite suddenly, all sensation of movement ceased. The pressure relaxed, and the motors faded away into silence as Maurice reached out a shaking hand to loosen the straps.

'David! Are we... are we through?'

'Through the Layer? Yes,' said Mellor, his voice harsh. 'Whether we've worked up enough speed to escape from Mars is another matter. You can loosen up, anyhow; if we're still moving at less than three miles a second, it won't much matter what we do. I can't give any more power.'

Maurice fumbled with the straps, and threw them off, pushing Bruce away. 'Phew! Who said you were a lightweight?' he said, and Bruce grinned as he floated upwards. 'I feel as though I'd been squeezed inside a vice. How soon shall we know?'

'The displays,' croaked Whitton, sitting up. 'I'm sorry - I tried to keep going...'

'It's not the displays I'm worried about,' muttered Mellor. 'Even though the Layer had cleared to a great extent, it was still powerful enough to put most of the registers out of action. Knight's hurt - see to him, one of you. Leslie, do you feel up to helping me with the repairs?'

'I can manage,' said Yorke weakly, opening his eyes and blinking. 'If we have not reached escape velocity by now, David what then?'

'Then we shall fall back,' said Mellor in even tones. 'We've power enough to make necessary course alterations and to carry out the landing manœuvres for Earth, but with six men aboard and the Violet Layer to contend with, we haven't much chance of making a safe landing back on Mars. I might manage it; but frankly there would be little point and I think on the whole I'd rather get it over and be done with it.'

Maurice clenched his teeth. Bruce looked calmly at him, and somehow Maurice felt reassured. Fate had played some queer tricks on them during the last few months, but he could not believe that they could fail now, at the very last moment.

'It's the subsidiary circuitry, I think,' said Mellor, his voice utterly without expression. 'All we want to know now is our speed relative to Mars. If it's greater than 3.1 miles a second, we've escaped; if not, we haven't.

Bruce, see what you can get out of the navigation. You should be able to get a good distance check.'

Bruce nodded. Whitton staggered up and thrust himself across the cabin to the unconscious Knight; only Maurice had nothing to do, and for him the next few moments were almost unbearable. For all the emotion they showed, Mellor and Yorke might have been making some casual experiment in a terrestrial laboratory, but he did not need reminding that they were working upon a problem that meant life or death.

'All right,' said Mellor at last. 'That was the trouble, sure enough. Link it up, Leslie, and we'll see.'

Yorke fumbled with the cabling. Maurice fastened his eyes on the numbers on the screen; he felt Bruce's hand on his shoulders. They all watched, and they all held their breath. Slowly, very slowly, the digits crept up. One mile a second... two... two and a half... The numbers stopped, and Maurice bit back a cry. Then, suddenly, the display jumped, and the digits carried on increasing. Three miles a second... four...

Mellor drew a deep breath, and passed a hand across his forehead. Only then did he show any signs of the strain of the last few minutes. 'Over four miles a second,' he said. 'We've done it - we've passed through the Violet Layer, and we've made our escape from Mars. Nothing can stop us now!'

CHAPTER 14

HOW IT ENDED

MAURICE SIGHED comfortably, and stared out of the window across the grounds of Woomera, squinting at the glare of the sunlight as it caught the white concrete buildings and lit them with dazzling brilliance. He could hardly believe that he was back on Earth, where the sky was clear blue and not mauve, and where he could see trees and grass, instead of the eternal orchre dust surface of Mars.

The journey back from Mars had been calm enough; 'as easy as a space-trip can ever be', as Mellor had said. For the first few weeks, the face of the Red Planet had dominated the scene, its ochre deserts and white polar caps finely displayed. Once, when Maurice had gone outside the *Ares* in his space-suit, he had even seen the dark tract of the Deltaton Sinus where they had found the *Hermes*, and he had waved idiotically with his gloved hands. Gradually, Mars had dwindled into a mere point, and once more they were 'in the wilds';

then, with agonizing slowness, the Earth had begun to
swell, changing from a star-like dot first into a tiny disk,
and then into a great, bluish-green globe. The
continents had taken form; Eurasia first, then the
Americas and then Australia, until Maurice fancied that
he could make out the desert which contained Woomera
itself. The word 'desert' had a different meaning now,
but he knew that in spite of all its unfriendliness and all
its perils Mars still held a strange fascination for him, so
that one day he must return.

He knew something about the landing procedure.
The Earth's dense air, so vital to all forms of life, was
an actual disadvantage now. The slightest error of
judgement, and the *Ares* would have plunged too deeply
and too quickly, until the friction heated its outer hull to
such an extent that the space-craft would have ended its
career in a streak of fire. Too shallow an angle, and the
Ares would have bounced off the atmosphere into
space. But Mellor and Yorke were well alive to the
dangers; and in any event as they approached the Earth
Woomera had begun to pick up the telemetry from the
Ares and help in guiding the space-ship home.. Just as
they had done above Mars, they had altered the course
of the *Ares* until they were running almost parallel to
the uppermost atmosphere, and then had ventured
downwards - slowly at first, making two complete
orbits of the Earth before dropping down into the denser
strata below. Once the motors had faltered at a critical

moment, and Mellor and Yorke had exchanged a sharp look; then the whine rose again, and at last the *Ares* was under full control, her stumpy wings extended so that she could be handled in just the same manner as the Space Shuttle. After that it had been 'plain sailing', and they had come to rest at last in the midst of the special wide and very long landing strip at Woomera itself.

Maurice pulled himself together. He was seated in Station Headquarters. Bruce was by his side, and Sir Robert Lanner stood by the centre table, accompanied by Mellor, Yorke, Whitton, Knight - now fully recovered from the effects of his injury - and most of the other Department Chiefs of Woomera. This was a special meeting, but Maurice had not been paying much attention to what had been said. His mind was millions of miles away, among the dust-hills of Mars.

'What are your final conclusions, then?' he heard Sir Robert say. 'From what I can gather, the position that you managed to send us, Dr. Yorke, was considerably in error, so that but for using Deimos as a mirror the rescue party would have had no chance of locating you in time.'

Leslie Yorke nodded. 'That is so. As we came down through the Violet Layer, we received an even worse buffeting than the *Ares* did. By some miracle our navigation systems escaped, otherwise we shouldn't be here; but all the other main computer systems were put out of action entirely, or severely damaged, and by the time we realized that things were badly wrong there was very little we could do about it. I couldn't regain altitude, so I had to land as well as I could, even though I was pretty sure that I'd wreck the *Hermes* in the process. I only wish we knew the exact cause.'

'The Violet Layer...' began Axel Haller.

'Oh, there's no doubt that the Layer is responsible,' said Professor Whitton thoughtfully. 'It's undoubtedly magnetic, but there's more to it than that, and it was sheer luck that it happened to clear away for long enough to allow us to pass through on the return journey. Even so, it was touch and go.'

'Suppose it hadn't?' asked Bruce, shrewdly. 'What would we have done then?'

'We'd already talked that over,' said Yorke simply. 'There would have been only one course. Mellor was needed to pilot the *Ares*, and so one of us, either Knight or Whitton or myself, would have had to stay behind. With five men only in a second launch, the chances of success would have been enormously increased.'

Mellor grinned. 'I wish I'd known what you were up to. I'd soon have told you what I thought of that scheme.' He paused. 'What really intrigues me is the fact that we found fossils - and pretty advanced ones at that.'

'Yes,' said Professor Whitton, 'and - I can't be sure - but it looked almost humanoid. Hardly a 'Martian' - but... All I am saying is that it is a great deal more advanced than I'd have expected. I wonder! Can there have been a real civilization? If so, it must have died out millions of years ago, when the seas dried up and the air leaked away. But I mean to know, and next time I go back I have every intention of finding out.'

'It can wait, anyhow,' said Yorke with decision, and stood up. 'I'm not good at making speeches, David, so I won't even try to thank you for what you've done, but you can well imagine what we all feel about it.'

Mellor grunted. 'Why single me out in particular? Those two over there had a hand in it as well, you know. If it hadn't been for them, I should have been utterly helpless.'

'I know,' said Yorke. 'The fact that one of them happens to be my own nephew makes me even happier. Incidentally, young Maurice, we've got to work out some plans for you. You're still only seventeen - you ought to be at school!'

Maurice laughed out loud. 'Lord! It'd seem a bit tame, wouldn't it? No, I think I'd rather stay here, if you'll have me. I want to see Mars again before I die.'

'It's not my decision,' said Yorke thoughtfully. 'Still, I've been talking it over with Sir Robert, and under the circumstances I think we can... er... fall in with your wishes, particularly as your friend Bruce seems anxious for you to join the team here. Don't imagine you'll be whirling spaceward again in a week or two. It's all work and not much play at Woomera, as you ought to know by this time, but I've no doubt that between us we can put you on the right track.'

Maurice looked at Bruce, and grinned. He felt very content.

- THE END -